Fan Club

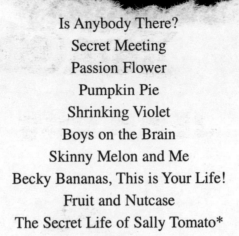

*Also available on tape, read by John Pickard

www.jeanure.com

Family Fan Club

JEAN URE

Illustrated by Karen Donnelly

HarperCollins *Children's Books*

First published in hardback in Great Britain by Collins 2000
First published in paperback in Great Britain by Collins 2001
This edition published 2004
HarperCollins *Children's Books* is a division of HarperCollins*Publishers* Ltd
77-85 Fulham Palace Road, Hammersmith,
London, W6 8JB

The HarperCollins *Children's Books* website address is:
www.harpercollinschildrensbooks.co.uk

3

Text copyright © Jean Ure 2000
Illustrations copyright © Karen Donnelly 2004

ISBN 0 00 717237 0

The author and illustrator assert the moral right to be
identified as the author and illustrator of the work.

Printed and bound in England by
Clays Ltd, St Ives plc

for Linda

one

"CHRISTMAS WON'T BE Christmas without any presents," sighed Jasmine, stretched out on the rug.

"*What?*" Laurel's head shot up from the magazine she was looking at. "What are you talking about?"

"Christmas," said Jazz. "Without any presents." She sighed again, rather more dramatically this time.

"N–no presents?" Daisy's lip quivered. "No presents at all?"

Solemnly, Jazz shook her head.

"Who said?" demanded Laurel.

"Nobody said." That was Rose, just a tiny bit scornful. How easily people allowed themselves to be taken in! "She's winding you up."

"You mean we will have presents?" said Daisy, hopefully.

" 'Course we will!" Jazz rocked herself into a sitting position. "Got you going, didn't I?"

Daisy was still looking bewildered.

"Oh!" Laurel's face cleared. "It's from Mum's play!"

"Opening line! *Little Women… 'Christmas won't be Christmas without any presents'*. I thought everybody knew that," said Jazz. But she and Rose were the only two who really read books, and Rose's were usually big fat learned volumes all about history. Rose was what Jazz privately thought of as "eleven-going-on-a-hundred". Took life just so-o-o-o seriously. Thought novels were a frivolous waste of time.

Laurel was the opposite. She only read film and fashion mags. As for Daisy – well! A smile curved Jazz's lips. It would be kindest to say that Daisy struggled. *Tries hard* was what the teachers always wrote on Daisy's school reports.

"You are all so ignorant," said Jazz.

"*I* knew it was the opening line," said Laurel. "I remembered it from the film."

"You ought to read the book. The book is far better."

Laurel pulled a face. "The book's old-fashioned."

"So?"

"So I like things that are new!"

"No soul," grumbled Jazz. "I suppose you'll say Mum's play isn't as good as the film."

"No, I won't, 'cos Mum's in it and it wouldn't be kind."

Mum was playing the part of Marmee. She had been rehearsing all through December, ready for opening on Boxing Day. Of course they were all going to see it, even though it was "way out in the sticks", as Jazz called anywhere that wasn't London.

"If it had been in the West End," mourned Laurel, "she'd be making a fortune."

"Not a fortune," said Jazz. "You never get a fortune, working in theatre. You have to do films and telly for that."

Their mum had been on telly, once. She had been in a soap called *Icing on the Cake*, all about a woman who ran a business making wedding cakes. Mum hadn't been the actual woman, but she'd been the woman's best friend. It had run for four years and Mum had been famous. Well, quite famous. Famous enough to be recognised in the street and for people to come clamouring for her autograph.

For the first time that any of them could remember there had been money in the Jones household. No more scraping and pinching and worrying about how to pay the bills. No more searching for clothes in the local Oxfam shops. No more hand-me-downs or cast-offs. Instead, it had been meals out and shopping in Marks & Spencer and FUN. They had even moved from their dark dingy flat in Dartford (out in the sticks) to a real house in London. It was admittedly only just in London. South London. But it was on the tube, said Jazz, and so it counted.

Icing on the Cake had been axed at Easter and now the money was starting to run out.

"We're going to be poor again," wailed Laurel, who was the eldest and could remember very clearly what it had been like before Mum was on the telly. Laurel really hated being poor. Jazz declared bravely that there were other things in life besides money, and Daisy was an undemanding little creature. So long as she had her cats, she was happy. Rose just muttered about the evils of *isms* – sexism, racism, classism – and made everybody groan. They always groaned when Rose started on what Jazz called her spouting.

"I hate it when you can't have the things you want," said Laurel. She meant clothes. Laurel loved to look smart and wear the latest gear. "If only Mum could get on telly again!"

Little Women was the first real job that Mum had had since *Icing*. They had held a conference, the five of them, to discuss whether she should accept it.

"It'll mean me being out in the evenings," warned Mum. "But we do need the money and Marmee is a good part."

"When I was little," said Jazz, "I used to wonder what Marmee meant!" She giggled.

"What does it mean?" said Daisy.

Laurel said kindly, "It's the American way of saying Mummy."

"They say *mommy*," explained Jazz. "Only it comes out" – she adopted an exaggerated American drawl – "as *marmee*."

Daisy nodded and went back to grooming Tinkerbell, their white cat. Tink was big and fluffy and Daisy spent many contented hours combing out the knots with his special cat comb. None of the others had the patience.

"I need a whole new wardrobe," said Laurel. "I wouldn't be seen dead in half the stuff I've got!"

"Yes, and I want acting classes and Daisy wants another kitten and Rose – well, I don't know what Rose wants."

"Nothing." Rose said it grandly. "I don't want anything."

"Just as well, since you probably won't get anything."

"You mean we're *really* not having any presents?" Daisy's face crumpled. "Not even stocking fillers?"

"Oh! Well. Yes. I expect we can run to those. But nothing big."

"A kitten isn't big."

"Kittens cost money."

"No! I know someone whose cat's just had a litter! They're giving them away *free*."

"Honestly!" Laurel shook her head. "You've already got Tink and Muffy! What do you want another one for?"

"I just love them so," said Daisy.

Rose said, "She needs something to cuddle."

"Cats *are* very cuddly," agreed Jazz. "Especially that great fat lump of a Tinkerbell."

"I'd sooner have Dad!"

The words seemed to come bursting out of Daisy before she could stop them. There was a silence.

"I thought we'd agreed," said Jazz, "that we wouldn't talk about Dad."

"I can't help it!" sobbed Daisy. "I miss him! I want him!"

"We all miss him," said Laurel. But it was true that Daisy had been Dad's girl. He had always had a specially soft spot for his little Daisy.

"Maybe he'll come home for Christmas," suggested Rose.

"Well, he won't," said Jazz, " 'cos I asked Mum and she said it was all over between them and we'd got to get used to the idea."

"That needn't stop him coming back for Christmas." Rose could be stubborn. She also enjoyed arguing. "He doesn't have to *stay* with us."

"No, but I don't expect he could afford the air fare." Laurel said it sombrely. "It costs a bomb."

Dad had been in the States for almost six months, now, looking for acting work. So far he'd only found what Jazz called bit parts. Bread-and-butter parts. Spits-and-coughs. Last time he'd rung he'd told them proudly that he was going to be in a Mel Gibson movie – "But it's a blink-and-you'll-miss-me kind of thing. Know what I mean?"

"It's so unfair!" cried Jazz. "Dad's a really brilliant actor!"

"There probably aren't that many parts for English actors in the States," said Laurel, sadly.

"Specially not *black* English actors." said Rose. Who else?

"Oh, don't start on politics!" Jazz turned on her, crossly.

"It's not politics," said Rose. "It's a fact of life. It's why he couldn't get work over here. 'Cos they don't use black actors."

Jazz opened her mouth to argue – and then closed it again. If she said, "They do," then it would be like saying Dad just wasn't good enough. But he was good! Even Mum said so, and Mum wasn't on speaking terms with him at the moment.

On the other hand, if she agreed with Rose… Jazz bit her lip. That would mean there wasn't going to be much of a chance for *her* when she grew up. Jazz couldn't accept that. She was going to be an actress, she was going to be a success, she was going to be a *STAR*.

"They do use some," she muttered.

"Oh! *Some*. Just a few. Just as tokens."

"Not always!"

"So when did Dad ever get a real part? I mean a *real* part? You tell me!" said Rose.

"Look, you two, just give it a rest!" begged Laurel. "It's incredibly boring when you go at it like that. I get sick to death of all this political correctness stuff."

"It's not p—"

"Oh, stop it! Just stop it!" Laurel clapped her hands to her ears. "If you don't stop I shall scream!"

There was a pause.

"Know what I think?" said Rose.

Jazz rolled her eyes. "No, but go on! Tell us."

She would have done, anyway. There was no stopping Rose when she got on her soap box.

"I think Mum and Dad should never have got married. I think it was doomed to failure from the word go. That's what I think."

Jazz stared at her, aghast. "Now you're being racist!"

"I'm not being racist! All I—"

"You are! You sound just like Nan! She's always going on about mixed marriages."

" 'Tisn't what I meant," said Rose.

"So what did you mean?"

"If you'd just let me *talk*, instead of jumping down my throat all the time, you wouldn't have to ask. What I *meant*," said Rose, "was that Mum being an actress and Dad being an actor was just a fatal combination. They almost never stay together, actors and actresses."

Jazz fell silent. She couldn't think of any argument against that.

"I suppose it wouldn't have been quite so bad," said Laurel, "if Dad had been the one to get into a soap."

Jazz whipped round. "Why not?"

"Well—" Laurel hunched a shoulder. "Women don't seem to mind so much. Men don't like it when their wives get famous and make a lot of money. Something to do with male pride," she said.

"Especially when Nan kept going on," agreed Rose.

"But Mum never did!"

"I don't see why they had to fall out about it," muttered Jazz.

"People always fall out when they're married. I'm going to stay single," said Rose.

Jazz resisted the temptation to inform her sister that she probably wouldn't have much choice in the matter, because what man would ever want to marry her with that mouth? Daisy was rocking to and fro with Tink cradled in her arms, and her face was puckered in distress. Mum and Dad breaking up had been harder for Daisy than for anyone. Part of the reason they had agreed not to talk about Dad was that it always ended in tears.

"This will be the first Christmas we've ever had without him." Daisy whispered the words into Tinkerbell's fur.

Rose frowned and turned away. Jazz and Laurel exchanged glances. They had promised Mum that if she accepted the part of Marmee, they would take care of Daisy. Mum was worried about Daisy. When Dad had left, she had wept almost non-stop for a week. Even now, if she got too wound up she was capable of crying herself into a state of exhaustion. Daisy wasn't as robust as the others. They all missed Dad, of course they did! But life had to go on.

"Just remember," said Jazz, bracingly, "it'll be far

worse for Dad than it is for us… we're at home and we've got each other. He's all by himself in a foreign country."

"*Jazz!*" Laurel kicked hard at her sister's ankle. Trust Jazz! Trying to be helpful and simply being tactless. As usual. If anyone could put their foot in it, Jasmine could.

Jazz seemed suddenly to realise what she had done. Hastily, putting her other foot in it, she said, "Well, no, actually, come to think of it, Dad will probably have a ball! I bet he'll be going to all the Hollywood gigs and meeting all the big stars… Mel. Al. Leonardo."

"*Leonardo!*" Laurel went into a mock swoon. Leonardo DiCaprio was the current love of her life.

"Imagine Dad getting to meet all those famous people!" enthused Jazz. "He probably won't miss us at all!"

Rose threw up her hands. Laurel said, "Of course he'll miss us! And he'll miss Daisy more than anyone. But he'll try not to be sad, because people shouldn't be sad at Christmas, and he won't want us to be sad, either. And he'll call us Christmas Day, like he promised, and Daisy can have first talk."

"And last one, too," said Rose.

"And last one, too. So you'd just better start thinking of things to say to him!"

"Make notes, I would," said Rose. "In case you forget."

Daisy liked that idea. She scrubbed at her eyes.

"I will!" she said. She scrambled to her feet, still hugging Tinkerbell. "I'll start thinking straight away!"

As Daisy left the room, Laurel looked at Jazz and tapped a finger to her forehead. "Dumbo!"

She meant Jazz, not Daisy, but Jazz's thoughts were already elsewhere. They never stayed still for very long.

"Hey! Know what?"

"What?"

"I just thought of something!" Jazz sprang up, excitedly. "Something we could do… we could copy some of the pages from Mum's script and act out a scene for her on Christmas Day!"

There was a silence.

"What for?" said Rose.

"For fun!"

"I wouldn't think it was fun," said Rose.

"Yes, you would, you'd enjoy it! Once you got started."

"Don't want to get started."

"Oh, don't be such a gloom!" Jazz took a flying leap on to the sofa and sat there, hugging her knees to her chin and rocking to and fro. "Think of Mum! She'd love it! You know she's always saying the things she likes best are the ones we've really worked at, like when we make our own cards."

"So we'll make our own cards," said Rose.

"We'll make our own cards *and* act out a scene. It will be like a present from us all."

Rose pulled a face. Laurel shook her head. There wasn't any arguing with Jazz once an idea had taken hold of her. She bounced up off the sofa.

"I'll go and start copying right now!"

"Can't," said Rose. "Mum's got the script with her."

"Then I shall make up my own one, from the book!"

"How are you going to copy it?" yelled Laurel, as Jazz scudded through the door. "Nobody can read your rotten writing!"

Jazz stuck her head back in again. "Not going to write! Going to use the typewriter."

"That old thing!" said Rose.

They had discovered the typewriter up in the attic, when they had moved in. It was very ancient. It had strange old-fashioned metal keys that rattled, and which you had to bash really hard, and an inky ribbon made of cotton that kept winding itself back every time it reached the end of the spool. To make copies you had to use carbon paper, which was messy, especially if you had to correct mistakes. Even messier if you put the carbon paper in the wrong way round.

"It's ridiculous," said Rose. "Why can't we have a computer?"

Jazz's head, which had disappeared, popped back in again.

" 'Cos we can't afford one!"

"It's like living in a cave," grumbled Rose. "Sometimes I'm surprised we've even got a *television*!"

Of all of them, Rose was the only one who was technologically minded. It was Rose who discovered how to use the video and Rose who learnt all the programmes on the washing machine. Mum was useless, and Dad hadn't been much better. Imagine having a dad who didn't know how to work the video!

Imagine having a *dad*. Jazz blinked, rapidly, as the tears came to her eyes. Sometimes even now, when she thought about Dad, great waves of misery would wash over her. They had all tried so hard to be brave about it, when the Great Row had happened and Dad had gone storming out. They had heard it from the upstairs landing. One by one, first Jazz, then Laurel, then Rose and Daisy, clutching Tink in her arms for comfort, had come creeping from their rooms and crouched, tense and shivering, at the head of the stairs.

It wasn't the first time Mum and Dad had shouted at each other. Jazz had always tried explaining it to herself by saying, "Well, they're actors. Actors are like that. They enjoy making a noise." But this time she had known, they had all known, that this was the big one. The Great Row.

It was about money, as usual. Before Mum had got into *Icing* they had rowed about the fact that they hadn't got any. They had rowed about whether they should both continue to pay their Equity fees and their fees to Spotlight, the actors' casting directory, or whether only one of them should. They had rowed about whether one of them should give up acting and do something else. Get a proper job. They had rowed because Mum had got her hair done for an audition and Dad had said it was a waste of money, and because Dad had a new publicity photograph taken and Mum had said it wasn't necessary.

They had rowed because they were worried. Because they couldn't afford to pay the bills or find a decent place for the family to live.

And then Mum had got into *Icing* and the money had come rolling in and they *still* had rows. Still about money. Mum had wanted to do one thing with it, Dad had wanted to do another. And instead of talking it out calmly and sensibly, they had ended up yelling. One time Mum had yelled, "Who's earning this money, I'd like to know?"

Jazz had thought that was very unfair. It wasn't Dad's fault he couldn't find work; it certainly wasn't for want of trying.

But then another time Dad had accused Mum of behaving like a prima donna, "Just because you're in some second-rate soap!" And that wasn't fair, either. Fame had never gone to Mum's head; she'd still been the same old Mum.

But perhaps, looking back on it, thought Jazz, Mum hadn't been as kind to Dad as she might have been. It couldn't have been easy for him, seeing Mum become a household name while he was still just an out of work actor.

On the other hand, Dad could have tried a little bit harder to be happy for Mum and not to show that he was feeling hard done by.

Maybe Rose was right, thought Jazz, sadly, as she toiled up the attic stairs, clutching Mum's old childhood copy of *Little Women*. Maybe actors and actresses oughtn't to get married to each other.

When I am an actress, she thought, I shall marry someone boring and sensible who works in an office and earns money and won't be jealous when I am rich and famous. We won't yell and shout and upset our children by storming out and saying good riddance. (Which was what Mum had screamed when Dad had gone.) We shall stay together *always* and be a proper family.

By the time she reached the attic, Jazz had difficulty seeing through her tears. She brushed them away, angrily. Jazz didn't like crying, not even when she was on her own. She certainly wouldn't do it in front of people. She was the strong one of the family.

But never mind Christmas not being Christmas without any presents, she thought. How could Christmas be Christmas without any dad?

two

"IT'S SO DREADFUL *to be poor*," sighed Laurel, "*looking down at her old dr—*"

"Stop!" Jazz waved her script, in anguish. "You don't have to say that bit!"

"What bit?"

"Looking down at her old dress. That's a stage direction! It's something you're supposed to *do*."

"Oh. Well, how was I to know?" said Laurel, aggrieved.

"The bits in brackets are what you *do*. The other bits are what you *say*. You'd think," grumbled Jazz, "that you'd know that by now. You've seen enough scripts!"

"The scripts I've seen never looked like this," said Laurel.

```
LivinG Rooom, MARch household
     Jazz is lying on; the rug
Jazz Chritsmas wonT be Chritsmas
     witout any presnets.
MEG  (sisghs) Its so daredful to be
     poor (looking dwon at her old dresss)
```

"I can't help it if the typewriter isn't any good," said Jazz. "Just get on with it! Rose, say your line."

"*I don't think it's fair for some girls to have plenty of pretty things and other girls having nothing at all.* Well, it isn't," said Rose. "But that's what happens when you live in a capitalist society."

"Do you mind?" Jazz glared at her sister. "Just say the lines! Don't add bits."

"Well, but this Amy person does my head in," said Rose. "Why do I have to play her?"

"Because I'm the director and that's who I cast you as!"

"But I'm nothing like her," said Rose.

"You're the youngest!"

"So what? It doesn't make me *like* her."

"Look, just shut up!" said Jazz. "You're supposed to be acting. *Injured sniff*. Give an injured sniff!"

Rose did so.

"That was good," said Jazz. "Daisy! Your line."

"*We've g–got f–father and m–mother and e–each other*," read Daisy, haltingly, from her script.

"Vomit," said Rose. "This is really yucky!"

"It's not, it's lovely!" said Jazz. "Don't be so horrid! It was Mum's favourite book when she was young."

"I cried buckets when I saw the film," said Laurel.

"You would." Rose looked at her eldest sister, pityingly. "The only films you ever like are weepies. And sickies."

"I don't like sickies!"

"Yes, you do! You just love it if it's about someone getting ill and dying. You *wallow*."

"Oh. I thought you meant sick like people going round murdering people. I don't like it when they go round murdering people. I l—"

"*Look!*" Jazz, impatient, stamped a foot. Daisy jumped. "Are we rehearsing *Little Women* or are we having a mothers' meeting?"

"Rehearsing *Little Women*," said Daisy.

"Thank you! That is what I thought we were doing. Can we please get on with it? We've only got four days!"

They staggered on, through the script that Jazz had so laboriously typed out on the old machine in the attic. Rose kept saying *Vomit* and *Yuck* and "I'm going to be sick!" Laurel didn't pay proper attention and kept reading stage directions and typing errors.

"*Really, girls, you are both to be balmed* – balmed? Oh! You mean blamed. *You are both to be blamed, beginning to lecture in her* – oops! Sorry! Stage direction. *You are old enough to leave off such boysih* – BOYISH *tricks and tobe have better.* What's tobe have b – oh! *To behave better.* Why do you keep splitting words up all funny?"

"I couldn't help it," said Jazz. "It's the typewriter. It keeps sticking. If you would just *concentrate*—"

"It's all yuck," said Rose.

Daisy was the only one who really tried, but Daisy wasn't the most brilliant reader at the best of times. It was as much as she could do to read what Jazz had actually typed.

"*If J–Jo is a r–romboy*—"

"A romboy!" Rose threw up her hands in delight. "Jo is a romboy!"

Jazz screamed, "Tomboy, you idiot!"

She wasn't screaming at Daisy; you didn't scream at Daisy. It was that stupid Rose, always trying to be so clever.

"What's the matter with romboy?" said Rose. "I like it!"

"It's w–what it says," stammered Daisy.

"Look, look! What's this word here? *Clotehs*." Rose wrapped her tongue round it, lovingly. "Meg wants some new clotehs!"

"So do I," said Laurel. "I want a whole wardrobe of new clotehs."

"We could invent a language," said Rose. "Typing Error language. Like sock would be cosk and milk would be klim and b—"

"All right! If you don't *want* to give Mum a present" – Jazz hurled her script across the floor – "then don't give her one!" And she raced from the room, slamming the door very loudly behind her.

There was a silence.

"We could call it Terrol," said Rose, brightly.

"Call what?" said Laurel.

"The language. Typing Error language… Terrol! Book would be boko. Foot would be foto. Hair w—"

"Stop it," said Laurel. "We've upset her."

"W–was it my fault?" whispered Daisy.

"No! Of course it wasn't." Rose rushed fiercely to her sister's defence. "You only read what she'd typed. You weren't to know!"

"We shouldn't have fooled around," said Laurel.

Laurel was, after all, the eldest. She was fourteen. Old enough to know better.

"Well, she's only got herself to blame," said Rose. "Takes everything so *seriously*."

Rose was a fine one to talk. Get her started on one of her *isms* and she had about as much sense of humour as a shark with a sore tooth.

"Anyway," said Rose, "she's not really doing it for Mum. She's just doing it to show off!"

"It's not showing off." You had to be fair to Jazz. It was true her enthusiasms sometimes ran away with her and made her a bit domineering, but she wasn't a show-off. "It's very important to her," said Laurel, "being an actress."

"Yes, 'cos she really really wants to go to drama school," said Daisy. "She wants to show Mum what she can do."

"Don't see how she thinks we can afford drama school if we can't even afford proper Christmas presents!" retorted Rose.

"She doesn't mean fulltime," said Laurel. "Just that little one up the road… Glenda Glade, or whatever it's called. There's a girl in her class goes there. Pinky Simons? The one with all the hair? She goes there twice a week. She's done a commercial. It's very frustrating," said Laurel. "It's what Jazz wants to do more than anything in the world!"

"What, a commercial?" muttered Rose, but she was starting to look a bit shamefaced.

"If she got a commercial," said Laurel, "she'd probably earn enough money to pay for herself."

"Huh!" Rose didn't mean to sound cynical, but how often had she heard Mum and Dad say the very same thing? *If I could just get a commercial…*

"Well, I know," said Laurel, reading Rose's thoughts. "But she can dream!"

Rose sighed. "I s'pose we'll have to do it for her. Even though," she added, with a flash of spirit, "we'd never be *cast* as Little Women. This was America! We'd probably have been slaves!"

"Oh, don't start!" begged Laurel. "Daisy, go and tell Jazz we're sorry."

"Why me?" said Daisy.

" 'Cos you're the only one she won't get mad at!"

Jazz was upstairs in her bedroom. She lay face down on the bed. Great sobs were shaking her, choking her, making it difficult for her to breathe.

Partly they were sobs of sheer rage. It was all so unprofessional! Messing up a rehearsal like that. How could they do such a thing? Rose and Laurel were the worst offenders. Poor little Daisy, she'd done her best. Daisy always tried to please. But those two—

Jazz banged her clenched fist into the pillow. They just didn't care!

Fresh tears came spurting. Tears of self-pity, as well as rage. They knew how much it meant to her, being an actress! They were deliberately ruining her chances. If Mum could just see what she could do, what she could *really* do, not just pottering round in the chorus of the school nativity play, she would surely let Jazz go to drama school? Only two days a week! It wasn't much to ask.

A timid knock came at the door. Jazz sprang into a sitting position, snatching up her sleeve for a handkerchief. She blotted angrily at her eyes. What had got into her, just lately? She never cried! She was the strong one. Now, it seemed, the least little thing set her off. She wouldn't normally let Rose and Laurel get to her. It must be something to do with Christmas, and Dad not being there. She couldn't imagine Christmas without Dad!

"J–Jazz?"

It was Daisy's voice, piping uncertainly. Jazz scrubbed at her eyes, blew her nose, stuffed her handkerchief back up her sleeve. She marched across to the door.

"What do you want?"

Daisy's lip quivered. "They told me to c–come and s–say sorry."

31

"Why you?" said Jazz. "You didn't do anything!"

"They r–really are s–sorry," whispered Daisy.

"Just too cowardly to come and tell me themselves!"

"They're scared you'll be cross with them."

"Well, I am," said Jazz. But Jazz never stayed cross for long. She rushed up to the boil, and then just as quickly simmered down. (Unlike Rose, who could nurse a grievance for days.)

"They want you to c–come and s–start rehearsing again."

"Only if they're going to behave themselves," said Jazz.

Rose and Laurel promised humbly that they would. Well, Laurel promised humbly. She said, "It was mean of us and we were stupid and I'm sorry. Let's start over! This time I'll concentrate."

Rose couldn't quite manage to be humble. She said, "I'll *try*. But I'm no good at acting and I can't get it together with this Amy person… not with *any* of them. They're all so twee and geeky!"

"They are a bit goody-goody," said Laurel. She said it apologetically, not wanting to upset Jazz.

"Did you think they were goody-goody in the film?" demanded Jazz.

"Well – y–yes. Sort of. But it was all right in the film!"

"Why was it all right in the film and not all right now?"

"Dunno," said Laurel. She shrugged. "Just was."

"I'll tell you why it was," said Jazz. "It was because of the costumes. They were all dressed up in old-fashioned clothes, so you didn't mind. You expect people in old-fashioned clothes to be a bit goody-goody. Like... you know! Going to church and saying grace and not swearing, and stuff like that."

"And girls behaving like *girls*," said Rose. She screwed up her face. "All prim and proper."

"It's how they were in those days. But it doesn't mean they weren't real people! What you have to do," said Jazz, "you have to pretend that you were living then, not now."

"Maybe it would help if *we* had costumes," said Laurel.

"Yes!" Daisy clapped her hands. "Let's have costumes!"

"Well..." Jazz sounded doubtful. She hadn't planned on being quite so ambitious. If you'll be responsible for them—"

"I'll help, I'll help!" cried Daisy.

"What did they wear?" said Laurel. "Was it crinolines? We could make hoops out of bits of wire and put them under our skirts and drape bedspreads over them and wear our school blouses with some of Mum's big scarves and—"

"Now see what you've done!" said Rose. "You've gone and turned it into a full-scale production!"

"That's all right," said Jazz.

"It's not all right! I haven't got time for all this. *Costume* fittings. *Dress* rehearsals. *Read*-throughs. *Photo* calls. I have work to do," said Rose, all self-important.

"What work?" said Laurel.

"I'm writing a book, if you must know."

"A book? About what?"

"Please!" Jazz waved her arms. "If we're going to do it, let's get started."

"I just wanted to know what she could possibly be writing a book about."

"She can tell us later. Let's take it from the top! *Christmas won't be Christmas*. We're all sitting round the fire—"

"It's about a colony of ants, actually," said Rose.

"A colony of *ants*?"

"Look, *please*!" said Jazz.

"Sorry, sorry!" Laurel sank down, cross-legged, on the floor. Rose bumped down beside her.

"Different-coloured ants," she hissed. "Black ants, red ants, white ants, b—"

34

"*Christmas*," said Jazz, very loudly, looking hard at Rose, "*won't be Christmas without any presents*."

"Sorry," said Rose.

This time, they managed to get through all six pages of the script. It was Laurel who had the final speech.

"*No, it's the toasting frok*, sorry, fork, *with Mother's shoe on it instead of the beard*. Beard??? Oh, bread! Silly me!" Laurel giggled. "*With Mother's shoe on it instead of the bread*. Phew!" She fanned herself with her script. "Is that the end?"

"Yes, because that's where Marmee comes in."

"Thank goodness for that! I don't know how I'm supposed to find time to learn all these lines," said Rose.

"Learn them?" Daisy sounded startled. "Have we got to learn them?"

"Only if you can," said Jazz, kindly. "But don't worry if you can't."

"I won't," said Rose.

"I didn't mean you!" Jazz swung round. "I meant Daisy."

Rose heaved an exaggerated sigh, but she didn't try to argue. It was accepted in the family that Daisy was treated more gently than the others.

"Know what?" said Jazz. "We actually are quite like the girls in *Little Women*. We are!" she said, as Rose opened her mouth. "In spite of what you say."

"How?" said Laurel. "How are we like them?"

"Well, if you think about it… their dad's away from home—"

"Their dad's fighting in a war," said Rose.

"Yes, well, so's ours, in a way. Except he's fighting it against Mum. Trying to prove to her that he can make it as an actor. The point *is*," said Jazz, a touch testily, "he's away from home." She really couldn't stand it when people would insist on interrupting with their little niggles and nitpicks when she was off on one of her flights of fancy. "Their dad's *not there*. Right?"

Daisy nodded, rather tremulously.

"And they're all dead worried in case he doesn't come back."

Daisy's eyes grew big. Her lower lip began to tremble. Really! thought Laurel. Jazz could be so dumb at times.

"It's all right," she said, squeezing Daisy's arm. "He does come back, in the end."

"Oh. Right! Yes," said Jazz. "Soon as the war's over… he comes back to them. Wars don't last for ever! So. As I was saying. There's four of them, yes? Just like us. They live with their mum. They don't have much money—"

"Tell us about it!" said Laurel.

"I'm trying to, if you'd only listen! We're just the same as they are, only in another age. Meg's the oldest, right? And she really cares about the way she looks."

"She's mumsy," said Laurel. Meg was her part. She didn't think she wanted to be compared to Meg.

"She's not!" said Jazz. "She's pretty – like you. And she enjoys being pretty." Jazz warmed to her theme. This was what being a director was all about! Giving your cast something to work on. "She only gets mumsy when she gets married. Like you probably will."

"I will not!" Laurel was indignant. She was going to be a top fashion model. She wasn't going to get mumsy!

"Well, anyway, you're both pretty," said Jazz. Everyone acknowledged that if Rose was the brains of the family, Laurel was the beauty. "And you both like to wear nice clothes. You can't deny it! You're always going on about clothes."

"Clothes are important," said Laurel.

"Yes, but they're specially important to you. The rest of us don't care so much. Wouldn't bother me," said Jazz, "if I didn't ever wear anything but dungarees."

"Now you're making me sound like a fribble!"

"You're not a fribble. It just happens to be something you're interested in. We'd probably be interested, as well," said Jazz, "if we looked like you."

"Hm!" Laurel tried not to sound self-satisfied, but

she did like it when people told her she was pretty. "What about you?" she said.

"Me. Yes. Well," said Jazz, "I suppose I am a *bit* like Jo. I mean, I am quite ambitious—"

"*Quite?*" said Rose. "I thought you told us you were going to end up in Hollywood and be a megastar?"

Jazz grinned. "All right. I'm ambitious! And I know I can be impatient sometimes, just like Jo."

"Yes, and, you're definitely boyish," said Laurel, getting her own back for the mumsy bit. She wasn't ever going to get mumsy! She looked pointedly at Jazz's hair, cropped so close to her head it might almost have been a cap.

"I'm not a bimbo," agreed Jazz.

"Maybe you'll turn out to be a lesbian," said Rose.

Jazz picked up a cushion and threw it at her. Laurel shrieked, "Rose! Don't be so disgusting!"

"There isn't anything disgusting about it," said Rose. "What's disgusting about it? Honestly, you're so prejudiced! Anyway, if she's really like Jo she'll end up marrying some old man who could be her father. That's what I call disgusting."

"*Ageist!*" taunted Jazz; and for once Rose actually had the grace to look abashed.

"Just get on with it," she said. In spite of herself, she was curious to hear what Jazz would say when she got to her.

"OK. Well – Beth."

"Am I like her?" said Daisy.

"Yes, you are!" Jazz leaned across and gave her a hug. " 'Cos you're good and sweet and everybody loves you!"

Nobody argued with that. Daisy might be a whole year older than Rose, who had just started in Year 7 that term, but she was still everyone's pet and treated very much as the baby. She went to a special school, for children with learning difficulties. It wasn't that she was stupid; just that she couldn't learn as fast as other people. At Daisy's school there were only fourteen children in a class. At the comprehensive, there were thirty. Daisy couldn't cope with that. She had come home weeping every day because "big girls" had bullied her, so Mum had used some of her *Icing* money to pay for her to go to Linden Hyrst. That was one of the few times when Mum and Dad had been in agreement. They weren't having their little Daisy being bullied.

"So what about Amy?" said Laurel, putting the question that Rose had been dying to put for herself.

Oh! Amy and Rose are *definitely* alike. Self-opinionated, for a start – you are, Rose, so don't deny it!"

Rose wouldn't. She rather prided herself on having opinions and voicing them.

"*Vain—*"

"Vain?" Vain was something else! Rose's head jerked up in genuine outrage. How could Jazz accuse her of being vain? "I'm not pretty enough to be vain!"

It was true. Of the four of them, Rose was the only one who could be called *homely*. (Meaning plain, only it wasn't kind to say so.) She was bright, vivid, intelligent – almost a genius, her sisters thought, but not pretty. It didn't bother her. She left all the girly stuff to the others.

"You're still vain," said Jazz. "You are *vain* of your *brain*."

Laurel laughed and punched the air. "Yessssss!"

"You are," said Jazz. "But that's OK. We're all vain about something. Except Daisy!" she added, giving her another hug. "She isn't."

"I am a bit," said Daisy.

"You?" Jazz laughed. "What are you vain about?"

"My nose," said Daisy, pressing a finger against it. Daisy had inherited Mum's nose. Small and neat and just the tiniest bit tip-tilted.

"Well, I never knew that!" said Jazz.

three

"OH, NO!" CRIED Laurel. She banged down her fork and stared accusingly at Mum across the kitchen table. "Not *her* again!"

Her was an actress friend of Mum's, known to the girls as Queen of the Soaps, or Lady Jayne. Her real name was Jayne Crichton, pronounced Cryton. She could be quite snooty if anyone called her Critchton. She could be quite snooty about a lot of things. Modern manners. Modern speech. Modern diction.

"Speak up! Don't mumble! Everyone today has sloppy diction. No one *projects* any more. How do you think you're going to be heard in the back row of the stalls?"

Mum said she was an actress of the old school and they had to be patient with her.

"But why does she always have to come at Christmas?" wailed Laurel.

"Because she has nowhere else to go."

"Not surprised," muttered Jazz, twizzling her fork in a mound of spaghetti. "Who'd want her?"

"Jazz, don't be unkind!" said Mum. "It's only once a year. Try to be a bit charitable!"

But Jazz couldn't. None of them could, not even Daisy. Lady Jayne didn't like cats, which meant that Tink and Muffy had to be shut in Daisy's bedroom all the time she was here. Imagine having to shut your cats away at Christmas! Just for the sake of some sour old woman who did nothing but nitpick.

"She's not really sour," said Mum. "It's the business that's made her that way."

By "the business," Mum meant show business. Lady Jayne had spent her life making small appearances in soaps – *EastEnders*, *Coronation Street*, *Emmerdale*, *Icing*. She had been in them all. But only ever bit parts. Half a dozen lines if she was lucky. Now even that seemed to have dried up. Mum said it was no wonder she felt bitter.

"When I first worked with her" (years ago, before Mum and Dad had got married) "she was enormous fun!"

It was hard to imagine the Queen of the Soaps being fun. She was dried and withered and crotchety and she made their lives a misery. It hadn't been so bad when Dad was there. Dad used to pull her leg and tell her to chill out. Lady Jayne said that was sloppy speech.

"*Chill out?* Is that English? What is it supposed to mean?"

And Dad would wink at them and say, "Go sit in the refrigerator!" which made Daisy giggle and Lady Jayne sniff. Dad refused to take her seriously.

"I was hoping that this year she wouldn't come," grumbled Laurel.

"Why this year?" Mum said sharply.

"Well."

"Well what?"

"*Well.*" Laurel scowled. It was Jazz who said it for her.

"With Dad not being here."

"What difference does that make?"

"It's not fair!" Jazz burst out with it, passionately. "We can't have Dad but we still have to put up with her!"

43

"Just because your father chooses to spend his time in America that's no reason for leaving one lonely old lady on her own at Christmas."

"You mean, if Dad were back in England," said Rose, "he could come and be with us?"

Mum tightened her lips. "He's not back in England, so the question doesn't arise."

"But if he *was*—"

"I wasn't the one who sent him away!" Mum rose to her feet, sweeping dishes off the table and clattering them noisily into the sink. "It was his decision, not mine."

"So he could come back if he wanted?"

"Yes, if you didn't mind your mother ending up on a murder charge!"

"*Mum*." Jazz stared at her mum, reproachfully. Mum was always so dramatic! Way over the top, thought Jazz, severely. Up on a murder charge! What a thing to say.

"Mum turned from the sink, took one look at Daisy's stricken face and dropped to her knees beside her.

"Sweetheart, forgive me! I'm sorry! I didn't mean that. I just meant – well!" Mum gave a little laugh, not very convincingly, and swept her hair back off her forehead. "You know how your dad and I used to fight. You wouldn't want that again, would you?"

44

Daisy's thumb went to her mouth. A sure sign of tears to come.

"You wouldn't," said Mum, "would you?"

Slowly, Daisy shook her head. A tear trickled out of the corner of one eye. Mum sighed.

"You see, what it is," she said, "sometimes two people just can't get along no matter how hard they try. It doesn't mean they don't love their children! It means they *do* love their children, and that's why they decide to live apart. So they won't always be quarrelling and upsetting them."

We have heard all this before, thought Jazz. And it just isn't true! If people really loved their children, really, really, *really*, then they wouldn't always be quarrelling and fighting. At any rate, that was the way it seemed to her.

"Try to cheer up!" said Mum. She gave Daisy a squeeze. "In two days' time it'll be Christmas, and who knows what you might find under the tree?"

"I th–thought we weren't having p–presents," hiccuped Daisy.

"Not having presents? Who said that?"

"J–Jazz did."

"I didn't really," said Jazz. "I was being Jo from *Little Women*. But I didn't think we'd be able to afford expensive ones."

"No, we can't," agreed Mum. "But that needn't stop us having fun!"

"What, with the Queen of the Soaps?" muttered Laurel, gloomily, only she waited till Mum was running water into the sink and couldn't hear.

"We've got the play," mouthed Jazz.

Jazz had worked them hard on the play. Like true professionals – they weren't Mum and Dad's daughters for nothing – they had all set to and managed to learn their lines, even Daisy. Laurel, as promised, had concocted costumes. She had found a stack of wire coat hangers and turned them into hoops. Over the hoops they wore their longest skirts, with their school blouses demurely buttoned right up to the neck and one of Mum's large flowery scarves draped over their shoulders and tied, cross-wise. Jazz had been really impressed.

"Never mind being a fashion model," she told Laurel. "You ought to be a designer!"

"Well, maybe I'll be both," said Laurel, who was secretly rather impressed with herself. "It's just a pity you haven't got long hair. Short hair ruins the effect!"

"Can't be helped," said Jazz. "We can't afford wigs."

There was a pause.

"Mum's got a wig," said Laurel.

Jazz giggled. "But it's blonde!"

"We could always dye it."

"*Dye* it?" Bold though she was, even Jazz shrank from the thought of dyeing Mum's wig. It was what she wore for auditions when they wanted someone young and glamorous. It had cost a lot of money, that wig.

"Well, we could," said Laurel. "After all, it's real hair."

"What about the others?"

"They don't matter so much. You're the important one! You're the lead."

"Well, I'll just have to manage without," said Jazz. "It'll be a test of my acting."

On Christmas Eve, they put the presents under the tree.

In some ways," said Mum, "lots of little things are more fun than just one big one."

"Yes, they are," said Daisy, loyally. "They take longer to open."

"Who are these from?" said Laurel, taking out four brightly-coloured packages from the box where Mum had been storing them. "Oh!" A rush of colour burned her cheeks. "They're from Dad! And oh, look!" she cried, delving back into the box. "He's sent you one, as well!"

"Yes, I saw," said Mum.

"I know what these are," said Rose, shuffling envelopes like playing cards. "These are from Nan."

Nan always sent them money – new, crisp £20 notes. She lived in Malta, so they very rarely saw her. She hadn't approved of Mum becoming an actress and she hadn't approved of her marrying Dad and she hadn't approved of her having four children "without visible means of support". Nan always said that Dad ought to go out and get himself a proper job, which made Mum angry, even though she and Dad had quarrelled about money.

"Why should he be the one who's expected to go out and get a proper job and not me?"

In any case, as Jazz pointed out, acting *was* a proper job – when you could get it. Mum had worked six days a week, sometimes all day and half the night, while she had been in *Icing*. And sometimes in rep, she told them, when they were striking one set and putting up another, she had worked twenty-four hours without a break. Let Nan try saying that wasn't a proper job!

She was the only nan they had, unfortunately. Dad had been an orphan, brought up in foster homes. Jazz often thought longingly of how it would be to have a cosy, cuddly sort of nan like you read about in books. Carmel, her best friend at school, had a nan like that.

"We are so short on relatives," sighed Jazz, surveying the little mound of packets and parcels at the foot of the tree.

"Sorry, I'm sure," said Mum. "I couldn't help being an only child."

"Is that why you had the four of us?" said Rose. She didn't exactly say it accusingly, but she did sound rather stern.

"Well… not exactly," said Mum. "You can blame your dad for that. He w—"

"*Wanted a boy!*"

Jazz and Laurel chanted it together.

"Men are so grungy," said Rose. "I suppose it was him that chose all these stupid flower names for us?"

She only asked because she wanted to hear Mum say it.

"Yes, he used to call you his little flowers," agreed Mum.

"Vomit," said Rose.

Mum smiled. "It was rather sweet, at the time… oh, now, Daisy!" She pulled Daisy towards her. "Whatever is the matter, pet?"

"If we'd b–been b–boys," wept Daisy, "he m-might not have g–gone away!"

"Darling, it was nothing to do with you not being boys! It was me he stopped loving, not you."

"And you stopped loving him," said Rose.

Mum frowned.

"D–did you?" said Daisy.

"Which of you stopped first?" Rose looked at Mum, challengingly. "You or Dad?"

"It doesn't work that way." Mum patted Daisy on the head, then reached out a hand and began rather fussily to rearrange a rope of tinsel on the tree. "It's not that simple. Relationships are things that grow, like people. They change, like people. But gradually."

"Like one morning you wake up and say, hey, I just realised! I don't love this person any more? I'm just trying," said Rose, "to understand."

"It's not something I can really explain." Mum looped the tinsel over a branch. "It's something you have to discover for yourself."

"Not me!" declared Rose. "I'm never going to have a relationship."

"That would be sad," said Mum. "Even though it may not have ended happily, your dad and I had a lot of good times together. I wouldn't have missed it for the world! Apart from anything else," she reminded them, "it's given me four beautiful daughters."

Laurel preened. Rose said, "Vomit. I'm not beautiful."

"You're not when you pull faces like that," agreed Mum.

Rose immediately crossed her eyes, let her mouth go slack and her tongue loll out. Daisy squeaked, "If the wind changes, you'll get stuck like that!"

"Who told you that rubbish?" scoffed Rose.

Daisy hung her head. "It was Dad."

"It's still rubbish," muttered Rose.

Lady Jayne arrived in time for coffee on Christmas morning. She started complaining the minute she walked through the door.

"Do you know how much that cabbie had the nerve to charge me? Ten pounds! *Ten pounds!* For a fifteen-minute journey. Well, I'm sorry, I said, you're not getting any tip out of me, I said. You can like it or lump it. Daylight robbery!"

"Of course, they probably charge double at Christmas," said Mum. "I should have come and picked you up. You should have asked me!"

"No, Debs. My goodness, no! I wouldn't dream of it. You've got enough on your hands, coping with four children. These men!" Lady Jayne gave one of her famous sniffs. "Better off without them, if you ask me. Best not have anything to do with them in the first place."

"But then *we* wouldn't be here," pointed out Rose.

"And a great loss to the world that would be, I'm sure!"

Rose thought about it. "*Nobody* would be here. We'd all die out!"

"All right, clever clogs." Lady Jayne gave her a little push. "I can see where you're going to end up… Houses of Parliament, that's where! Spouting hot air along with the rest of them."

"I might well become an MP," said Rose. "It's something I've considered."

"Heaven help us!" said Lady Jayne.

Rose and Lady Jayne were always sparring with each other. Secretly, Jazz thought they rather enjoyed it.

Over coffee they listened to Lady Jayne's latest list of complaints. Mostly they were tales of how she had been done down or insulted.

She had gone for an audition for a commercial and been kept waiting over an hour and then been told she was too young.

"Too young! At my age!"

"Well, I suppose it's quite flattering, in a way," said Mum.

Jazz giggled, and hastily clapped a hand over her mouth. Lady Jayne said, "You can laugh, miss! You wait till you get to my age. And that's another thing! I went for this interview for a telly part. Director was there. I thought he was the tea boy. Looked about twelve years old. *Ms Crichton*, he says to me. *Ms Crichton, how much experience have you had?* Well! I told him, in no uncertain terms. I've had more experience than you've had hot dinners, sonny! That put him in his place."

"Did you get the part?" said Jazz.

"No, I did not, thank you very much for asking. Wouldn't have wanted it, anyway."

"So why did you go for the interview?" said Rose.

Mum cleared her throat, rather loudly. "I think we'll open the presents, now."

"Yessss!" cried Laurel.

"Daisy," said Mum, "come and help me give them out."

"For the next ten minutes all that could be heard was the rustling of wrapping paper being ripped and scrunched, together with glad cries of "Oh! Brilliant! Just what I wanted!" plus the occasional sniff from Lady Jayne, who always found it difficult to be pleased about anything.

"Oh! Look what Dad's sent me!" breathed Laurel, kneeling on the floor as she undid her presents.

"What is it, what is it?" Jazz craned to see.

"A signed photograph of Leonardo!" Laurel keeled over, dramatically, clutching the photo to her chest.

"Last of the big spenders," sniffed Lady Jayne. But Laurel couldn't have been happier.

"Wait till I show it at school! They'll be green with envy!"

"Well, whatever turns you on." Lady Jayne gazed down, distastefully, at the present she had just opened. What's this supposed to be?"

"It's from me." Daisy announced it, proudly. "I made it for you specially! I got one of those tubes that people put things in to send through the post, and I put pretty paper all over it and made a little handle so you can hang it up somewhere."

"But what is it *for*?" said Lady Jayne.

Daisy beamed. "It's to put plastic bags in. Instead of throwing them away… you put them in the tube."

"You *re-use* them," said Rose. "It's environmentally friendly."

"Oh. Well!" Just for a moment, Lady Jayne seemed at a loss. She sniffed. "That will help save the world," she said.

Well, it would, thought Jazz. If everyone recycled instead of chucking out, there would be a lot less litter cluttering the place up. Lady Jayne was always so *ungracious*. Daisy had spent hours making her presents.

"Girls!" Mum intervened, hastily, before Jazz could start anything. "What about this surprise you promised me?"

"Yes!" Jazz scrambled eagerly to her feet. "Wait there! We'll go and get ready."

"I don't know what it is, exactly" – Mum leaned across to Lady Jayne – "but it's something they've been working on."

Lady Jayne rolled her eyes. Miserable old witch! thought Jazz. We'll show her!

Jazz headed for the door, the other three hot on her heels. Laurel's bedroom, being the biggest, had been pressed into service as a dressing room. All their clothes were laid out neatly on Laurel's bed.

"And then for Jazz," announced Laurel, "there's this." She scrambled on to a chair and proudly lifted something down from the top of the wardrobe. Jazz felt her jaw drop open.

"That's Mum's wig!"

"Yes," beamed Laurel. "I dyed it."

There was an appalled silence. The wig, which had been honey blonde, the same colour as Mum's own hair, was now a pale sludge brown.

"Does Mum… *know*?" breathed Jazz.

"No, but it's all right, it'll wash out. At least—" Laurel seemed suddenly stricken with doubts. "I think it will. But even if it won't, she can always have it dyed back again! Let's put it on and I'll pin it up the way Jo would have hers."

Jazz had to admit, she certainly felt more Jo-like wearing Mum's wig. She just hoped Mum wouldn't immediately recognise it and start screaming. Because she *was* going to scream! Laurel had better be prepared.

Fortunately, being sludge brown and pulled back into an elaborate bun (Laurel quite fancied herself as a hairdresser) it didn't bear very much resemblance to Mum's wig at all. At any rate, Mum didn't immediately scream and cry, "Stop the show!"

"Oh!" She gave a crow of delight. "Charades!"

"Not charades," said Laurel. "It's a *play*."

"Even better!" cried Mum.

"And look, we've done programmes!" said Daisy, thrusting one each at Mum and Lady Jayne. "I did them," she added.

Daisy was proud of her programmes. She had written them out in her best handwriting, and decorated them with coloured flowers.

 LITTLE WOMEN

Act 1, Scene 1. Sitting room of March household. The four March girls are gathered round the fire.

Cast:

Jo	Jasmine Jones
Meg	Laurel Jones
Beth	Daisy Jones
Amy	Rose Jones

Produced & directed by Jasmine Jones
Costumes by Laurel Jones
Programmes by Daisy Jones

"Well!" Mum beamed, brightly, at Lady Jayne. "How exciting! I wasn't expecting this. Live entertainment on Christmas Day!"

Lady Jayne just sniffed. But no one took any notice of her; Mum was the one who counted. If only, prayed Jazz, Daisy could manage to remember her lines…

Miracle of miracles! Daisy did!

"I tried specially hard," she whispered to Jazz, as very solemnly, at the end, they took their bows. " 'Cos I know how much it means to you."

Mum and Lady Jayne both clapped.

"Bravo!" cried Mum. She jumped up and gave them all a hug, in turn. "That was wonderful, darlings. What a surprise! It was lovely!"

Even Lady Jayne seemed (just a little bit) impressed.

"Looks like there's another actress in the family," she grunted.

It was quite the nicest thing she had ever been known to say.

"Yes," agreed Mum, "Jazz is—"

It was as far as Mum got, for at that moment the telephone rang, loud and shrill, out in the hall.

"*Dad!*" shrieked Laurel, and went tearing out there.

Jazz is what? thought Jazz. It was so frustrating! Mum had already jumped up and followed Laurel into the hall.

"I don't think it can be your father," she was saying. It's far too early in the day."

"It's one o'clock!" squealed Daisy.

"Not in California. It's only" – Mum did some quick calculations on her fingers – "only five o'clock in the morning in California!"

But Laurel was holding out the receiver and beckoning urgently at Daisy.

"Quick, quick, it's Dad! Have you got your list?"

Mum raised one eyebrow after the other and went back to the sitting room. Daisy reached up her skirt and pulled out a scrap of paper. (Where had she been keeping it? In her *knickers*?) Timidly, she took the receiver. The other three clustered round, impatient for their turn.

Dad rang them once a month but they could never talk for very long. A minute each was the very most they ever had, which was why it was important for Daisy, who always got tongue-tied, to work out beforehand what she wanted to say. Today, perhaps because it was Christmas, Dad was splashing out. Laurel, who had grabbed hold of the receiver as soon as Daisy had finished, seemed intent on gabbling for ever. Agitated, Jazz tugged at her sleeve and mouthed, "Me!"

Laurel put her hand over the mouthpiece. "It's all right, we can talk as long as we want!"

Mum had come back out into the hall. She seemed surprised they were still on the phone.

"It's all right," said Jazz. "We can talk as much as we want."

Mum raised her eyebrows again and disappeared. She and Dad hadn't spoken once since the Great Row, except just occasionally when Mum had happened to pick up the phone and it had been Dad calling from the States, when Mum would say, "Oh. It's you. Hang on, I'll get the girls." Not even, "How are you?"

But then Dad never asked after Mum, either. Parents could be *so* uncivilised.

Jazz got her turn at last. She snatched up the receiver. "Dad?"

"Hi, baby!" Dad's rich, velvety tones came clearly down the line. It was hard to believe he was all those thousands of miles away. "What's all this I hear about playacting?"

Jazz launched enthusiastically into an account of *Little Women*, how she had written the script and Laurel had made the costumes and how even Daisy had managed to learn her lines.

"What I really, really want to do is go to drama school, you know? Just that little one up the road? Like if someone could wave a magic wand and—" Jazz stopped, and bit her lip. It wasn't fair, laying all this on

Dad. He didn't have a magic wand. Nobody did.

"Well, anyway," she said, "I think it was a success!"

By the time they had all had their turn at speaking, and Daisy, as promised, had spoken twice, they had been on the telephone for almost half an hour.

"Well! That will have cost a pretty penny," said Lady Jayne. "Come into a fortune, has he?"

"It's *Christmas*," said Laurel.

Lady Jayne sniffed. "Tell me about it!"

"So what's he up to?" said Mum.

"Er—"

Laurel turned, helplessly, to Jazz.

"He didn't say," said Jazz. She should have asked him! How could she have been so egotistical? Going on about herself all the time!

It seemed that the others had gone on about themselves, too.

"I guess we can take it he hasn't landed a part in the next Bruce Willis spectacular." Lady Jayne gave a self-satisfied smirk. She would hate it if Dad were suddenly to become a big star.

"He might have got a part," said Jazz. "Just because, he didn't tell us—"

"Oh, he'd have told you!" Lady Jayne nodded, smugly, and sat back in her chair. "He'd have told you, all right!"

Unfortunately, Jazz knew that that was probably true. If Dad hadn't talked about work, it meant that nothing had happened. He hadn't even talked about auditions or interviews.

"Well!" Mum stood up. "I have to say your play was absolutely brilliant. I'm really proud of you all! I'm sure your dad would have been, too."

"He was!" said Daisy. "I told him all about it. He said he wished he could have been here."

There was a silence.

"Yes. Well. How about you four going off to get changed?" said Mum. "I'll go and see to lunch."

Jazz trailed up the stairs after the others. She was still brooding over what Mum might have been going to say. *Yes, Jazz is* – what? *What?* Jazz is *what*? She had to know!

Jazz turned, and went bounding back down again. Mum was in the hall, punching out numbers on the telephone. 1_4_7_1. It was what you dialled to find out the last caller. But Mum knew the last caller! It was Dad.

"What are you dialling that for?" said Jazz.

"Oh!" Mum started, guiltily. "I just wondered where your father was ringing from."

"America," said Jazz. Where else?

"Well, anyway, they didn't have the number," said

Mum. "You were excellent as Jo, by the way. Really excellent. Well done!"

Jazz glowed. "Mum, do you think—"

"I know what you're going to ask me," said Mum. "I know you want to go to drama school. But Jazz, sweetheart, we simply can't afford it at the moment! Give me a while. Maybe something will turn up... some telly. A commercial." She laughed. "Even a movie! Just keep your fingers crossed. You never know what might happen. By the way—" Mum leaned forward, peering suspiciously through narrowed eyes. "What *is* that you're wearing on your head?"

four

MUM HAD BEEN rather cross about her wig. If it hadn't been Christmas, she blisteringly informed them, she would have been even crosser. She had been quite cross enough, as it was.

"What a thing to do! How utterly thoughtless and selfish!"

Jazz defended her sister by pointing out that while Laurel may have got a bit carried away, "It was all for the sake of the play!"

"You think that makes it any better?" fumed Mum.

Laurel declared that she was sorry, but "I was doing it for Jazz! She really wanted to impress you!"

Mum refused to be placated.

"You've ruined a perfectly good wig! Do you have any idea how much that wig cost?"

"It'll wash out," said Laurel, hopefully.

"Oh, will it?" said Mum.

"Well... it might," said Laurel. She was beginning to sound rather miserable.

"And if it doesn't?"

"You could always have it bleached back!"

Lady Jayne sucked her breath in.

"Let's go and give it a shampoo!" cried Daisy.

"I'm warning you," said Mum, "if it doesn't work I shall expect you to contribute your Christmas money for a new one!"

"Cheap at the price," sniffed Lady Jayne.

Two spots of colour appeared on Laurel's cheeks. She had been relying on Nan's Christmas money to buy herself some new tights and some make-up.

"Don't worry," whispered Daisy. "You can have mine!"

"I was only doing it for Jazz," muttered Laurel.

Jazz wrestled a moment with her conscience. Did that mean she ought to offer *her* Christmas money?

The moment passed. There wasn't any reason, Jazz decided, why she should be expected to make a sacrifice. Whatever Laurel might say, she hadn't really dyed Mum's wig just so that Jazz could impress Mum with her acting skills. She'd dyed it because she wanted her costumes to look their best. Which was perfectly understandable, but no concern of mine, thought Jazz. Besides, Jazz needed her Christmas money. She had started a drama school fund, which so far had only reached the pitiful amount of £8. Nan's contribution would bring it to £28, which was more like it. Twenty-eight pounds made you feel that you were getting somewhere.

They all clustered anxiously in the bathroom, watching as Mum doused her wig with shampoo.

"If anything will shift it, this will."

A great cheer went up as streams of sludge brown water gurgled down the plug hole.

"I told you, I told you!" crowed Laurel. "I'm not stupid! I knew it would come out!"

While Rose and Daisy laid the table for lunch, and Jazz gave a hand in the kitchen, Laurel rushed off with the wig to blow dry and style it. She came back down, beaming triumphantly.

"See?"

Laurel did have a way with hair. The wig was now smooth and gleaming.

"Not quite the same colour, though, is it?" sniffed Lady Jayne.

Laurel's face fell. "It a–almost is."

"It's honey brown," said Jazz.

"Oh." Lady Jayne curled her lip. "Is that what you call it?"

Laurel looked anxiously at Mum.

"It might suit you better like this," she said.

Mum tried it on. They held their breath.

"Well," said Mum. She turned this way and that, studying herself from all angles in the large mirror over the mantelpiece. "I suppose it's a new image," she conceded. Then she smiled. "Maybe it'll bring me luck!"

Danger averted! They let out their breath. Laurel hurled herself at Mum and threw her arms round her neck. Lady Jayne sniffed.

"You let them run rings round you. They're spoilt."

We're not, thought Jazz. We just have a wonderful mum! But they had a wonderful dad, as well. How come two such wonderful people couldn't get it together? It just didn't make any sense.

On Boxing Day, Mum's show opened and they all went to see it. Mum went off early, in the car, while the rest of them travelled down later by train. Lady Jayne came with them. She had a cold which she said she had caught from the cab driver (the one she had accused of daylight robbery).

"I don't see how you can have done," objected Rose. "Colds don't develop that fast."

"This one did," said Lady Jayne.

"But it can't have!"

"Well, it has. What do you know about it? Are you a doctor? That's right, you edge away, miss! You keep your distance!"

Jazz had wriggled herself to the far end of the seat. She didn't want to catch Lady Jayne's rotten cold! On Sunday she had an important party to go to. It was a showbiz party, given by a director friend of Mum's. He had said that Mum was welcome to bring Jazz and Laurel with her. Jazz had been looking forward to it for weeks!

Laurel had obviously remembered the party, too. She shuffled along the seat after Jazz. Rose, on the seat opposite, next to Lady Jayne, also shuffled. Only Daisy was left, trapped between Lady Jayne and the window.

I suppose it must look rather rude, thought Jazz, but she is spraying her germs absolutely everywhere. It was true that Lady Jayne was somewhat vigorous in her sneezing. First there came a long-drawn-out "Aaaaaaaaaaaaaaaaaah", during which she threw back her head, nostrils flared, nose pointing ceiling-wards, mouth gaping open. This was followed by a resounding "TISHoo!" like a great clash of cymbals. Sometimes she managed to catch it in her handkerchief, but quite often she didn't.

Laurel put her mouth close to Jazz's ear. "I hope she isn't going to do that all through the performance!"

I shall die if she does, thought Jazz. But Lady Jayne, for all her moaning and groaning, was just as much a pro as Mum and Dad. She could control her sneezes if she really wanted. Obviously, on the train, she was just being self-indulgent, for she sat through the entire performance of *Little Women* with no more than the occasional muted "Whumpf!" into her handkerchief.

It was exciting, standing in the foyer of the theatre and seeing a large glossy photograph of Mum, and on a poster, in big red letters, WITH DEBBIE SILVER AS MARMEE.

Silver had been Mum's name before she married Dad. In married life she was Mrs Jones. Jazz could never make up her mind, when she became an actress, whether she would be Jasmine Silver or plain Jasmine Jones. Silver was more glam, but Rose always said that Jasmine Jones had a ring to it. Rose could be right; she often was.

The girl playing Jo was called Keri Dunn. She was tall and slim with thick chestnut hair. Jazz couldn't help envying her. What she wouldn't give to be up there on stage in her place! Afterwards, Laurel said loyally that "She wasn't half as good as you," but Jazz wasn't quite sure whether she could believe her. She sometimes thought that Laurel said things just to be kind. But then Rose leaned over, under cover of the applause, and hissed, "You were far more convincing than she was! She's too *pretty*."

Rose almost never said things just to be kind. It cheered Jazz up, until she remembered that no matter how convincing she was, no one would ever dream of casting her as Jo. They wouldn't cast her as Ophelia, either. Or as Lady Macbeth. Or as Beatrice, in *Much Ado about Nothing*. Jazz wanted to play Beatrice almost more than anything in the world! There wasn't any reason why Beatrice shouldn't be black. Maybe one day…

"Hey!" She felt a finger poking her in the ribs. "Get moving!" said Laurel.

Lady Jayne led them to the pass door, which divided the world of make-believe from the world of reality. Backstage, all was hustle and bustle. Jazz could feel the blood pounding through her veins. This was where she belonged! This was her home.

On the way to Mum's dressing room they passed the girl who had played Jo. Keri Dunn. She didn't look quite as stunning offstage. Her skin was bad and she had a rash of pimples on her forehead. Jazz tried not to be pleased, but after all, she thought, I am only human.

Driving home in the car, with Lady Jayne in front with Mum and the four girls squashed up in the back, they discussed the performances. Everyone agreed that Mum had been brilliant as Marmee.

"You do a good accent," said Lady Jayne.

"Thank you kindly!" laughed Mum. "What did you think of our Laurie?"

Laurie was the Lawrence boy – the boy next door. Jazz said she thought he was OK, Rose that he was a bit wet. Daisy, always the most impressionable, thought that he was lovely.

"Not a patch on Leonardo," said Laurel. Everybody groaned.

"How about Jo?" said Mum.

"Nowhere near as good as Jazz," was the general verdict.

Lady Jayne sniffed, and sneezed, but she didn't actually argue. I *am* good, thought Jazz. I know I am!

"Now, are you sure you're going to be all right?" said Mum.

"Mum! I told you!"

Rose gave Mum a little push towards the front door, where Jazz and Laurel stood waiting. It was Sunday, the day of the party, and if Mum had asked once whether Rose and Daisy would be all right, she had asked a dozen times. She was anxious about Daisy, who had caught Lady Jayne's cold and was tucked up on the sofa, with Muffy and Tink. Daisy's colds were always worse than other people's. Once when she was little she had caught pneumonia and had to go into hospital, so Mum always fussed over her more than she did the others.

"You've got the telephone number?" she said.

"Yes, Mum! I've got the telephone number." Rose said it kindly and patiently, as she shepherded them down the hall.

"We shan't be long. Just a couple of hours. We'll be back by nine at the latest."

"*Yes*, Mum."

"If anyone comes to the door, don't open it. Not even on the chain!"

"*No*, Mum."

"Well, then." Mum smiled, brightly. "Are we ready?"

Jazz had been ready for over an hour. She liked to look neat, but she knew she could never be glam so she didn't try. She was wearing a crop top, bright orange, and a short black skirt with an orange border which showed off her legs. Jazz wasn't vain, but she was secretly proud of her legs. She considered them her best feature. (Even if a girl at school *had* once said she looked like a racing spider. Totty Langhorn, that was. Squat little gnome.)

"Laurel?" said Mum.

Laurel had come sailing down the stairs at the last minute. Laurel was someone who *could* look glam. She was wearing a blue dress that had been one of Mum's favourites until an awful day, just a few weeks ago, when she had discovered she could no longer get into it. She had blamed it on Dad. (Mum blamed everything on Dad.) She said that she had done nothing but "comfort eat" ever since he had left, which Jazz found odd since Mum always claimed to be glad that Dad had gone. Anyway, she had got too fat (not that anyone could call Mum *fat*) and so the dress had passed to Laurel. With a few nips and tucks it fitted her perfectly.

But how grown up she looks! thought Jazz. With her hair swept back, Laurel could almost have passed for eighteen. It made Jazz, in her crop top and short skirt, feel about ten years old.

"Have a nice time," said Rose, who didn't mind in the least not going with them. Rose quite liked being left at home, in charge. Dad always said that Rose was the one real adult in the family.

"The rest of us are all just children."

Mum was driving them to the party because that

way, she said, she wouldn't be tempted to drink. (She was on a diet and drink was strictly forbidden.)

"Can we drink?" said Jazz.

"Certainly not!" said Mum.

"But we're not on diets!"

"Can't help that."

"It'll seem so childish," sighed Laurel. "And there's bound to be champagne!"

"Too bad," said Mum. "Just think yourselves lucky you're coming at all."

The director giving the party was called Rufus White. He only lived twenty minutes away, in an old tall house near Clapham Common. Mum said that some people were going on afterwards to have dinner, but she hadn't wanted to do that.

"Why not?" wailed Laurel. "I'd love to go and have dinner!"

Crushingly, Mum said, "The dinner is for grownups. Not for children. You'll have your fun early on."

Just at first, Jazz wasn't sure that she was going to have fun. Mum disappeared almost immediately, swept away by an actress friend.

"Be all right, you two?" She beamed and nodded and vanished into the crowd, leaving Jazz and Laurel on their own clasping glasses of orange juice.

"There *is* champagne," whispered Laurel. "I saw it!"

Jazz shrugged. She wasn't interested in champagne, she was interested in people, only there didn't seem to be anyone else there of her age. There were several little kids racing about, all over-excited and showing off, and lots of what Dad called Beautiful Young Things, also over-excited and also showing off, shrieking and kissing and making a lot of noise. Jazz thought she recognised one of them. A girl dressed in deepest black with spiky hair and lips painted purple.

She wondered if she dared go up to her. Well, why not? she thought. It's a *party*.

Jazz took a breath.

"Excuse me," she said. She said it in her best voice. Polite and posh. Her actress voice. Not the one she used for school or with friends. Her Sarf Lunnon voice, as Dad called it. "Excuse me… were you on television the other day?"

The girl looked at her as if she were some form of low life that had crawled out of a drain.

"Who knows?" she drawled.

Well! I'd know if I'd been on television, thought Jazz. She felt a bit dashed. Maybe the girl was incredibly famous and thought that she had been insulted. Jazz swallowed, and turned back to Laurel – only to discover that Laurel was no longer there. She was being led across the room by a tall, floppy youth wearing a dinner jacket. I bet he thinks she's older than she is, thought Jazz. She wondered what to do next. She wasn't shy, but I've been snubbed once, she thought. I'm not going to be snubbed again!

She wriggled her way through a crush of people until she came to a bit of clear space. She stood there, clutching her orange juice and trying to pretend that she was having a good time. She had been so looking forward to this party! She had even had visions of being *discovered*. Of the great Rufus White catching sight of her and going, "Oh, my goodness, Debs! Is this your daughter? How would you like a part in my next production, my dear?"

That had just been plain silly, of course. That had been day-dreaming. Except that these things did happen! Just occasionally. Jazz tilted her chin and placed one leg carefully in front of the other. After all, you never knew who might be watching.

A tickle began to twitch in her nose. She sneezed. Heavens! She must have caught Lady Jayne's stinky cold. She sneezed again. She tried to do it in as ladylike a manner as possible. Not a big vulgar Aaaaaaaaaaaah followed by a clash of cymbals, but a little genteel t'shoo!

She sniffed and felt for her handkerchief. She hadn't got one! She hadn't got a handkerchief! Laurel, busy being – t'shoo – grown up, had brought a stupid little bag with her, but Jazz scorned such things. Now what – t'shoo! – was she supposed to do? She couldn't even wipe her nose on her sleeve because she didn't have any sleeves. And any – t'shoo! – way, it would be horribly inelegant.

Jazz stared round, despairingly, in search of Mum or Laurel. She couldn't see either of them! And now her nose was beginning to drip. She blotted it, on the back of her hand. Ugh – t'shoo! – disgusting!

"Want a rag?"

Jazz spun round. A boy was standing there, grinning and holding out a handkerchief.

"It's OK, it's clean," he said.

Jazz wouldn't have cared if it had been filthy dirty. She snatched at it, gratefully.

"Think I'm getting a cold."

"Really?" He leaned excitedly towards her. "Give it to me, give it to me! Breathe over me!"

"Are you mad?" said Jazz, blowing her nose.

"No, but I'm supposed to be doing a day's filming next week and maybe if I got a cold I wouldn't have to. My brother could do it, instead."

Jazz regarded him, in stupefaction. "You're loony!" she said.

"I'm not, I just don't want to have to do any more

filming. My dad keeps making me do these one-liners for him. It's really boring!"

Jazz swallowed. "Who's your dad, then?"

"Rufus White. Who's yours?"

"T.J. Jones."

"Is he an actor?"

"Yes, and so's my mum. She's Debbie Silver."

"Oh, yes. I know her. Are you an actress?"

"Not yet."

His lip curled. "I suppose you're a wannabee."

"No, I'm a gonnabee!"

The boy laughed. He was about the same age as Jazz. He wasn't terribly handsome – his hair was blond and a bit limp and his mouth was crooked – but he had bright blue eyes that crinkled rather nicely when he laughed. Jazz laughed back.

"Why do you think filming's boring?" she said.

"Dunno." He shrugged. "Just is. All that hanging around while they set the lights and sort out the camera angles, and then you have to do it over and over till you feel like screaming."

I wouldn't feel like screaming, thought Jazz. It seemed very unfair that someone who didn't want to act should be pushed into it, while other people – such as Jazz – couldn't even get to drama school.

"Why does your dad make you?" she said.

" 'Cos he doesn't feel comfortable working with kids and he knows he can shove me around. Did you come here to watch all the luvvies? *Wonderful* to *see* you, dwahling!" He screeched it in a high falsetto voice, hurling himself at Jazz and going, "Mwah! Mwah!" as he planted kisses on both cheeks.

She couldn't help laughing. Actors and actresses did tend to be a bit over the top, even Mum and Dad.

"Who is the girl with spiky hair?" she said.

"Dee Lovejoy. She's a cow."

"Cows are nice!" said Jazz.

"OK, so she's a slime. Is that your sister over there?"

Jazz looked where he was pointing and saw Laurel, standing with a group of Beautiful Young Things and gazing up, all melty-eyed, at the tall floppy youth in the dinner jacket. She was holding a glass in her hand and it didn't look like a glass of orange juice. She'll catch it if Mum sees her, thought Jazz.

"Mm." Jazz nodded.

"She's a lot older than you!"

"No, she isn't," said Jazz, bristling. "She's fourteen. She's just pretending to be older. Who's that boy she's with?"

"Simon Allsopp. He's another slime."

"Is he an actor?"

"No, he just happens to live next door. His mum and

dad are friends of my mum and dad. They're all slimes."

"Seems to you everyone's a slime," said Jazz.

"No, they're not! You're not."

Jazz felt a big stupid grin spread across her face, though why she should care one way or another what a not terribly good-looking boy with limp hair thought of her, she really couldn't imagine.

"What's your name, anyway?" he said.

"Jazz. What's yours?"

"Theo. Short for Theodore. What's Jazz short for?"

"Jasmine." Jazz pulled a face. "But nobody calls me that."

"Nobody calls me Theodore. I'd bash 'em if they did!"

Jazz spent the rest of her time at the party standing in a corner with Theo, giggling at his jokes and listening in amazement to the stories that he told her.

"Well," said Mum, as they drove home, "you seemed to be having a ball! That was Rufus White's son you were chatting up."

"Yes, I know," said Jazz. "He was funny. But his dad makes him act and he doesn't like it."

"Oh, he probably does," said Mum. "He was probably just trying to impress you. How about Laurel? Did she meet anyone interesting?"

Laurel didn't answer. She had fallen asleep with her

head on Jazz's shoulder. Her mouth was open and she was making little whiffling sounds.

"No?" said Mum.

"She met a boy called Simon," said Jazz. "But he's a slime!"

Definitely not orange juice, Jazz thought. Laurel was going to suffer for that in the morning!

five

"ALL RIGHT, THEN, you lot!"

Mum was getting ready to leave for the theatre. Christmas was over, and they were back at school, but Mum's play was booked to run until the end of February. Every day except Wednesday (when she had an afternoon performance) she would be there to say hello when they came home, then they would have tea together and Mum would listen to any of their problems before setting off.

It seemed they were all having problems, just at the moment. Daisy still had the remains of her cold and was whiny and grizzly. She kept complaining because Mum wouldn't let her have another kitten.

"They're so sweet! And they're *free*. They just want good homes for them."

Jazz was consumed with jealousy because Pinky Simons, who was in her class, had now started tap and ballet lessons as well as going to Glenda Glade two times a week.

"And she's useless! She's absolutely *useless*!"

Laurel moaned non stop about the state of her wardrobe. Even Jazz was sick of hearing about the state of Laurel's wardrobe. All her clothes (she said) were grotesque. She would sooner (she said) go about naked than wear some of the hideous dowdy old-fashioned *muck* that was hanging in her closet.

"How can I go out with Simon looking like a six year old?"

It was Simon who was at the root of it. Ever since meeting him at Rufus White's party, Laurel had given herself airs and graces. Looking down her nose at us, thought Jazz. Like we're just kids and she's grown up. But she isn't, no matter how she preens and prances!

Today it was Rose's turn. Rose was grumbling again about not having a computer.

"Look at all this stuff I have to write out… pages of it!" She pulled a wodge of paper from her school bag and banged it down on the table. "It takes me ages! Far longer than anyone else. They all have computers except me. It's not f—"

"Don't say it!" Mum held up a hand, like a traffic policeman. "Just *do not say it*. All I ever hear from you people is I want, I want, I want! It's about time you learnt that we can't always have everything we want. It's a hard fact of life, and there's nothing I can do about it. I'm sorry you don't have parents who can afford to indulge you, but that's the way the cookie crumbles. You'll just have to make the best of it. I'm sick of the lot of you!"

Mum swept up her bag and her car keys and headed for the door.

"I'm going off to the theatre. You four can sit here and whinge amongst yourselves. At least I shan't have to listen to it!"

Mum disappeared, slamming the door behind her. There was a stricken silence.

"Marmee never turned on her kids like that," muttered Laurel.

Maybe they didn't whine as much, thought Jazz. She said it aloud, but Laurel only tossed her head.

Rose said, "No, they were such *goody*-goodies."

"Now we know why Dad left," said Laurel. "Obviously couldn't stand Mum bawling him out all the time."

"Dad was just as bad," said Jazz, trying to be fair.

"Dad didn't yell and shout!"

"He did sometimes."

"Not as much as Mum!"

"No, but then he used to go all quiet and that used to drive her mad."

"Are you saying it was Dad's fault?"

"It was both of them! Both of them!" Jazz jumped to her feet and began snatching dishes off the table and clattering them into the sink. "And now we've upset Mum and it's not fair, 'cos she's doing her best!"

"I only wanted a kitten." Daisy said it pleadingly. "Just one dear little sweet kitten!"

"You're being greedy," said Rose. "You've already got Muffy and Tink. And anyway, kittens cost money. Yes, they do!" she said, as Daisy opened her mouth to protest. "You still have to feed them and take them to the vet. We can't *afford* another cat. We haven't *got* any money. We're *poor*."

"Not like we used to be," said Laurel; but the money Mum was earning from *Little Women* wasn't enough to keep them, and the money from *Icing* was dwindling fast. A few small cheques had dribbled in – repeat fees from telly work that Dad had done, royalties from a commercial he'd been in, and *Icing* had sold to Australia and New Zealand, but still it was hardly a fortune. Just enough to pay the bills while they all kept their fingers crossed and waited for the telephone to ring. It sometimes seemed to Jazz that Mum and Dad spent their lives waiting for the telephone – for that call from their agent to say they'd landed a big part, that Steven Spielberg wanted them for his next movie, that the National Theatre had asked for them. It hadn't happened yet, but one day…

"Maybe they *ought* to have gone and got proper jobs," said Rose.

"No!" Jazz howled it at her. Acting was what Mum and Dad had trained for; acting was what they did best. It was impossible to imagine them working in a shop or an office.

"In that case we'll just have to stop moaning," said Rose, as if she hadn't been one of the worst offenders. She gathered up her papers. "I suppose I don't *really* mind getting writer's cramp and wearing my fingers down to stumps."

Next day when they arrived home Mum was waiting for them with a broad smile on her face.

"Guess what? The telephone rang!"

"Dad?" squeaked Daisy.

"No, not your dad! It was Gus." Gus Manning was Mum's agent. "They want me for a telly part. I've got to go for an interview tomorrow. The only thing is—" She gave a little laugh, rather nervous. "It's to play the part of a thirty year old."

"Mum, no problem!"

They hastened to reassure her. After all, thirty, forty, thought Jazz; where's the difference?

"You can get away with it!"

"You'd pass for thirty any day!"

"You really think so?" said Mum.

"Absolutely!"

"You still look really young," said Jazz.

"Well, one can but try. I shall wear my wig," said Mum.

"You've got a new one?" gasped Laurel.

"My *honey brown* one," said Mum.

"Oh."

Laurel shut up after that. Jazz could guess what she was thinking: if Mum doesn't get the part, it will be all my fault for ruining her wig…

It would, too!

But the next day when they came in, the beam on Mum's face stretched from ear to ear.

"I got it! They didn't bat an eyelid. I thought they'd all pull faces and think, who's this old bag? But they offered it to me on the spot!" Mum giggled, happily. Jazz couldn't decide which pleased her more, being taken for a thirty year old or being offered a part.

"What is it? Who are you playing?"

"She's a high-powered executive. Her name's Amanda Lovejoy. It's two weeks' work, starting from next Thursday. If I decide to take it."

"*If?*"

"We need the money!" said Rose.

"Yes, I know we do. But it would mean I'd be out all day filming and then all evening at the theatre. I'd hardly ever see you!"

Daisy's lips quivered. Quickly, before she could go and ruin it all, Jazz cried, "We'll be all right! We can manage. You can't not do it, Mum! It's your career!"

"But I'm not sure whether you can be trusted by yourselves," said Mum. She looked rather hard at Laurel as she said it. Laurel had had the hugest of hangovers after the party. She had felt so ill it had frightened her. She had confessed to Mum that she had drunk "just a tiny little sip" of champagne, though later she had admitted to Jazz that she'd had four glasses.

"It tasted so lovely! It was all bubbly."

She had added, however, that she didn't think she would be drinking it again.

"If I go ahead," said Mum, "can I have your solemn sacred word that you will all behave yourselves?"

They promised that they would.

"And you'll look after Daisy for me?"

"Of course we will!" said Jazz. They would never let any harm come to Daisy.

"All right, then," said Mum. "I'll do it!"

Would the part of Amanda Lovejoy bring in enough money for just two days a week at drama school? Jazz couldn't help wondering, but thought perhaps it wasn't quite the right time to ask. Best to wait until Mum had been paid!

"My God, what are you wearing?" screeched Jazz.

It was Saturday evening, and Laurel had appeared at the top of the stairs, a vision in scarlet.

"That's Mum's dress!" She was wearing Mum's dress. Just to go out with mouldy old Simon!

"I know," said Laurel. "I've borrowed it."

She stepped down in a stately manner and gave a little twirl. Rose and Daisy came running out to see.

"What have you done to it?" gasped Rose.

"Nothing very much. Only tacked up the hem. It'll easily untack again. And I've used safety pins for taking it in. They don't show, do they?"

Bemused, Jazz shook her head.

"I told you I wouldn't be seen dead in anything I've got."

"You're wearing Mum's earrings, as well!" said Daisy.

"Yes." Laurel put up a hand and flicked at them. "They're nice, aren't they? All sparkly."

"But how have you fixed them?" said Jazz. "Your ears aren't pierced!"

"I've fixed them with wire. You can't see 'cos I've curled my hair over."

Jazz swallowed. Laurel hadn't just curled her hair over, she'd puffed it up like a big froth of candy floss. She had also plastered her face with make-up. All this for smarmy Simon!

"You'd better be home on time," said Rose. "You know the rules!"

Laurel smiled, a sweet sickly smile. "Simon will bring me home. He's got his dad's car. Oh, and there he is!" she cried, as a car horn tooted. "See you later!"

Really, thought Jazz, Laurel had become horridly slurpy just lately. If this was what having a boyfriend did to you, then she was glad she didn't have one. She didn't count Theo, even though he had rung her up several times and taken her out once – to the Theatre Museum in Covent Garden, with free tickets. But Theo wasn't a *boy*friend: he was just a friend. And that was the way Jazz meant to keep it. She didn't have room in her life for slurpiness.

They stood watching at the window as Laurel went wobbling down the path to the front gate. Jazz saw that she was wearing high heels. *Mum's* high heels. No wonder she was wobbling! They were the gold strappy sandals Mum kept for special occasions. The heels were like long spikes, about three inches tall. If she's not careful, she'll break her ankle, thought Jazz. Laurel really had become quite impossible!

As they watched, smarmy Simon stepped out of the car and came round, with a flourish, to open the passenger door. *Creep!* thought Jazz. He was, she supposed, quite handsome in a nerdy sort of way. If you went for that sort of thing. All long and bendy with a beaky nose that made him look like a startled parrot, and black hair scragged back into a soppy little scrawny pony tail, and—

At that moment, Simon turned and smiled and waved a languid hand, and in spite of herself, Jazz had to gulp and swallow. It was a good thing she wasn't as easily impressed as her sister! Laurel probably saw the slimeball as being tall and slim and aristocratic-looking. Like an eagle, or a Roman emperor. She probably thought it romantic to have black hair tied in a ponytail. It probably gave her the flutters when he spoke in that slow, drawling voice of his. There was no accounting for taste.

As Laurel stepped into the car, Simon bent and dropped a light kiss on her forehead.

"Ugh! Yuck!" said Daisy. "He kissed her!"

It was too disgusting, thought Jazz. Laurel had only been out with him a couple of times.

"What does she *see* in him?" wailed Daisy.

"She thinks he's tall, dark and handsome," said Jazz.

"And posh," said Rose.

"And posh," agreed Jazz.

"She finds him *attractive*. Ugh! Yuck! Throw up!" said Rose.

Jazz sighed. "She thinks he's sophisticated."

"Just because he's older than she is!"

"How old?" said Daisy.

"Well, he's at uni," said Jazz, "so he must be at least eighteen."

"Daisy's eyes widened. "That's *old*."

"That's why she likes him."

There was a silence.

"I suppose she knows what she's doing," said Rose.

"I s'pose so," said Jazz. But in any case, Laurel was the eldest. She wouldn't take any notice what the rest of them said.

The car drove away. Jazz and Rose went upstairs to their bedrooms, Jazz to practise audition speeches (just in case she was lucky enough ever to have an audition),

Rose to write an essay for school. Daisy settled herself in front of the television to watch her favourite video, *Lady and the Tramp*. She had seen it at least a dozen times, and it always made her cry, but as she said, "It ends happily, so it's all right."

At nine o'clock, Jazz came back downstairs in search of something to eat. Practising audition speeches made a person hungry.

"Want anything?" she said to Daisy.

Daisy shook her head. "I can't find Tink," she said.

"He's probably in the garden."

"He isn't! I've looked. And anyway, it's raining. He hates the rain!"

"In that case he'll be hiding somewhere. Cats aren't stupid," said Jazz. She helped herself to a glass of milk and an apple and wandered through to the sitting room.

"Let's watch *Little Women*."

Daisy obediently sat down on the sofa. Jazz slotted the video in and sat down next to her, with her milk and her apple. Almost immediately, Daisy was up and on her feet, running across to the window.

"What are you doing?" said Jazz.

"I thought I heard him!"

"Look, just stop fussing," said Jazz. "You know what cats are like."

"But they shouldn't be out at night! It's dark, he'll get run over!"

"Not if he's hiding under a hedge, he won't."

At ten o'clock on the dot Rose came charging downstairs.

"She's not back yet!"

In all the bother of Daisy, fretting herself over the missing Tinkerbell, Jazz hadn't realised how late it was. Mum would be home in an hour's time! What was she going to say if Laurel hadn't turned up?

"Ten o'clock," said Rose. "That's her deadline!" She looked at Daisy. "Why have you been crying? I suppose it's that stupid film!"

"It's n–not the film." Daisy sniffled, and wiped her nose on the back of her hand. "T–Tink's not here."

"Neither's Laurel," said Rose. "That's more to the point! If Mum comes back and finds—"

She broke off as the telephone rang.

"I'll get it!" Jazz leaped out into the hall and clawed up the receiver. "Hallo?"

"Jazz? It's me!"

"*Laurel*. Why aren't you home yet?"

"He won't bring me!" Laurel sounded scared. "We're at this horrid p–party and he won't l–leave and I th–think people are t–taking drugs. I don't know what to do! I haven't any m–money and I d–don't know how to get home!"

"What is it, what is it?" Rose was jigging impatiently at Jazz's elbow.

"It's Laurel," said Jazz. "Smarmy Simon won't leave the party and she doesn't know how to get home."

"Where is she?"

"Where are you?" said Jazz.

"I d–don't know!"

"She doesn't know."

"She must know!"

"You must know," said Jazz.

"I don't! I think it's somewhere in the c–country."

"She thinks it's somewhere in the country," said Jazz.

"Oh, for goodness' sake!" Rose snatched at the receiver. "Laurel? Don't be so useless! Go and ask someone. Get the address!"

Jazz was impressed, in spite of herself. Good old Rose! Dad was right: she *was* the only adult in the family.

They waited.

"She's gone to ask someone," said Rose. "Find a pen!"

Humbly, Jazz did so.

"Write it down… 26 Chestnut Grove, Wimbledon. What's the telephone number?" Rose relayed it to Jazz, who meekly made a note of it. "Right. Now we're going to think of something," said Rose. "You just wait there and we'll ring you back when we've thought." She put the receiver down and turned to Jazz. "So what are we going to do?" she said.

Jazz took a breath. She was the next oldest, after Laurel. Rose was the youngest, she couldn't leave it all to Rose.

"We've got to get her back before Mum comes in! We promised," said Rose. "We said we could be trusted!"

They had given their word. And then that wretched Laurel had to go and get all gooey-eyed over a smarm like Simon and end up stuck, at ten o'clock on a Saturday night, in the middle of nowhere. Not that Wimbledon was nowhere, exactly. And it wasn't the country, either, though maybe it might look like it if the house was on the Common.

"We've got to do *something*!" said Rose.

"I know, I know!" Jazz stamped a foot. "I'm thinking!"

"Well, you'd better think quickly, or—"

"I know," said Jazz. "I'll ring Theo!"

Theo was only thirteen, the same age as her, but he was streetwise. He had been around, he had acted on television. He would know what to do.

Jazz picked up the receiver and punched out his

number. Please, God, let him be there! Please, God! Let him—

"6428."

"Theo!" cried Jazz.

"I told you he was a slimeball," said Theo, when Jazz had explained the situation. "Hang on, I'll go and talk to Dad."

Within seconds, he was back.

"It's all right," he said. "Dad'll go and pick her up. What's the address?"

Jazz read it out to him. "And please," she begged, "could you ask him not to tell Mum?"

"I'll tell him he's not to," promised Theo.

"Well," said Rose, "what it is to have friends in high places."

"Theo's not in high places," said Jazz. But she supposed that he was, in a way, having a dad who was a television director. Television directors were a bit like gods. They were the ones who had the power to give you work.

Jazz suddenly turned and scudded back upstairs.

"Where are you going?" yelled Rose.

"Just thought of something!"

What Jazz had just thought was that she had better make sure she was looking her best for when Rufus White turned up. You never knew… he might be in the middle of casting something right now!

From downstairs, as she raced along the landing to her room, she heard the sound of Rose's voice, somewhat irritable.

"Look, just stop carrying on! He'll turn up. He always does!"

For a moment, Jazz hesitated. Daisy loved those cats! Well, they all did. But Daisy was the real cat person. It would break her heart if Tink were to have got run over.

Well, he wouldn't have got run over! He was just on the prowl. Being a cat. Doing his own catty thing. Cats were always going walkabout. Jazz hardened her heart. She had her career to think of!

Ten minutes later, clad in a clean top and a new pair of jeans, she joined Rose in the sitting room.

"Did he say how long it would take?" said Rose.

"Didn't seem to think it was too far."

"Mum will go ballistic if she finds out... daring to disturb the great Rufus White!"

"Well, what else could we have done?"

Rose hunched a shoulder. "Could've told her to call a minicab, I s'pose."

"But that would cost the earth!" Jazz certainly wasn't raiding her drama school fund just to rescue Laurel from the consequences of her own folly. Anyone could have seen that smarmy Simon was a slimeball.

"Where's Daisy gone?" she said.

"Dunno. Upstairs, probably."

Jazz heaved a sigh. She went to the foot of the stairs and called up: "Daisy!"

No reply. She tried again, louder, this time. "Day-zee!"

Still no reply. Bother! That meant she was in one of her states. That was all they needed! Mum coming home to find Daisy in a state.

Jazz bounded up the stairs, three at a time, and into Daisy's room. It was empty.

"Daisy!"

She raced back down and into the kitchen: the kitchen was also empty.

"Dai—"

She stopped. Who had taken the chain off the front door?

"Oh, God!" cried Jazz. "She's gone!"

"She's what?" yelled Rose.

"She's gone!"

"Gone where?" Rose came out into the hall.

"Gone to look for Tink! And it's pouring with rain!"

"Oh, really," said Rose, crossly.

"It's our fault! We should have helped her!"

"Well, what with *Laurel*," said Rose.

"Yes, but you know what she's like. You stay here! I'll go and see if I can find her."

98

Jazz tore out into the rain. "Daisy!" she cried. "Daisy, where are you?"

She ran up the road one way, she ran up the road the other way. The rain lashed down; within seconds she was soaked.

"*Daisy!*" she screamed.

Mum and Dad would never forgive her if anything happened to Daisy. Jazz would never forgive herself! Daisy was fragile; she needed someone to take care of her.

"DaiZEE!"

From out of an alleyway, a small figure emerged: sodden and trembling, clutching a bundle of fur.

"Daisy!" Jazz ran towards her.

"I found him!" Daisy smiled tremulously at Jazz through her tears. "He was in someone's garden!"

Sheltering from the rain, thought Jazz. He would have come home, in his own good time – but not before Daisy had sobbed herself into a state of exhaustion.

She put an arm round her sister's shoulders and hurried her back up the road. They arrived at the house at the same moment as Rufus White pulled up in his car, with a subdued Laurel sitting beside him.

"Here you are!" he said. "All safe and sound!"

And Jazz with the rain running in rivulets down her face, and her feet squelching in her shoes…

But who cared about squelchy feet? Who cared about Rufus White? Daisy was the main concern!

"Quick, quick!" Jazz hustled her sister up the path. "Someone run a bath!"

"Why? What's happened?" Laurel raced after them, tottering perilously on her high heels. "Why are you all wet?"

"They've been out in the rain," said Rose, snatching Tink away from a shivering Daisy. "Looking for *this*."

"Without an umbrella?" shrieked Laurel. "Without a raincoat? Without—"

"Daisy – take – your – clothes – off – I'm – going – to – run – a – bath!" cried Jazz, pelting up the stairs.

"Mum's going to be furious," said Laurel. "Letting *Daisy*, of *all* people—"

"Oh, shut up!" snapped Rose. "You've caused enough trouble for one evening!"

They had just the time to bundle Jazz and Daisy's clothes into the dryer and out again before Mum arrived back. Daisy, fresh from her bath, all warm and pink in her dressing gown and nightie, was happily cuddled on the sofa with Tink.

"What a picture of bliss," beamed Mum. "All's well, I take it? No problems while I've been away?"

"No problems," said Jazz.

"One, two, three… where's number four?"

Number four was upstairs in her bedroom, frantically hiding Mum's dress and shoes in the recesses of her wardrobe. It wasn't until they had all retired for the night that she appeared, like a wraith, at the side of Jazz's bed.

"Now what's the matter?" said Jazz.

"Something awful." Laurel's face crumpled. "I've lost one of Mum's earrings!"

six

"Where's Laurel?" said Mum. It was eleven o'clock on Sunday morning, and Laurel hadn't yet put in an appearance. "Why is she still in bed? What's she been up to?"

"She went to a party," said Rose. "*With Simon.*"

"Oh, *did* she? I hope she hasn't been drinking again."

Daisy giggled.

"It's not funny," said Mum. "We've all been there, we've all done it – but not at fourteen years old, thank you very much!"

"It's all right," said Jazz. "She swears she's never going to touch drink again, ever."

"Yes, I've heard that before," said Mum.

"I think she means it," said Jazz. Laurel was in enough trouble as it was. "I'll go and wake her!"

Jazz galloped up the stairs in her usual fashion and burst unceremoniously into Laurel's bedroom.

"Wake up, wake up, you lazy slug!"

Laurel ungummed a bleary eye.

"I've only just gone to sleep," she said. "I've been awake all night, worrying." She wriggled into a sitting position, clutching the duvet round her. "How am I going to tell Mum?" she whispered.

"I don't know." Jazz regarded her sister with a mixture of exasperation and pity. Laurel had been stupid, no doubt about that. She had brought it all on herself. But then, if you were in the throes of love, thought Jazz, striving to be broad-minded, it probably frazzled your brain.

"Mum's going to be so mad at me!" wailed Laurel. "They were her favourite earrings!"

"They were the ones Dad bought for her," said Jazz. "The time he got that film part. When he went to Spain." Dad had come home loaded with presents for all the family. Mum had scolded him for spending his hard-earned money.

Laurel suddenly brightened.

"Maybe she won't mind that I've lost one!"

"Why? Just because they were from Dad?"

Laurel nodded, happily. "She probably won't ever want to wear them again. She mightn't even notice they've gone!"

"You must be dreaming," said Jazz.

"Well, then, she might think she's gone and lost them herself."

Jazz sucked in her breath. "That would be the meanest thing ever!"

"What?" Laurel lay back, sullenly, against the pillow. Not telling her?"

"Yes, 'cos just suppose one day she and Dad make it up and Dad says where are those earrings I got you and Mum goes to look for them and they're not there… he'd think she'd got rid of them!"

There was a silence.

"D'you really think they'll ever make it up?" said Laurel.

"Well… they might," said Jazz.

"But Mum says she doesn't ever want to see Dad again!"

"People say things like that. They don't always mean them."

"Mum does!"

"How do you know? She might just be saying it 'cos she's hurt."

"So what am I going to do?" bleated Laurel.

"If you really want my advice," began Jazz, and then stopped as Rose's voice came bellowing up the stairs.

"Jazz–it's–Theo–on–the–phone!"

"Wait there," said Jazz. "I'll be back."

Laurel groaned. When Jazz and Theo got talking, there was no stopping them. Laurel couldn't imagine what they found to talk about. She and Simon hadn't really talked at all.

Simon was hateful! She didn't want to think about him. And she most *certainly* wasn't ever going out with him again.

She burrowed back down beneath the duvet. Perhaps she could go into a decline, like Victorian women used to. She would just stay in bed and gently fade away. Anything would be better than facing Mum's wrath!

Jazz was back again almost immediately. Laurel heard her bounding up the stairs.

"You've gone to sleep again!"

"Don't feel well," mumbled Laurel.

"Stop being cowardly! You're just trying to avoid things. If you want my advice—"

Laurel wasn't at all sure that she did.

"If you want my advice, you ought to go to Mum and

throw yourself on her mercy. You should say, I'm deeply humbly sorry, I've behaved like a total idiot, I lost my heart to slimy Simon." Jazz clasped both hands to her bosom. "I gave him my love and he let me down."

Laurel stared at her, revolted. "I can't say that!"

"Why not? It's true," said Jazz. "You went completely gaga over him. I told you he was a slimeball! Anyhow—" She yanked at the duvet. Laurel screeched, and yanked it back. "It's all right, you don't have to hide," said Jazz. "You've been lucky. Guess what?"

"What?"

"Theo's found the earring! It was in his dad's car."

"Oh!" Laurel gave a great squeal of joy and jumped out of bed. She hurled herself at Jazz. "Thank you, thank you, thank you!"

"He's going to bring it round right away, so if you really want to slurp over anyone," said Jazz, shoving at her sister, "you can slurp over him."

"No!" Laurel shook her head. "I'm through with men."

"Until the next time," said Jazz.

"There isn't going to be a next time! Oh, I do hope Mum doesn't want to wear her earrings before he gets here!"

Since Mum had just finished washing her hair and was in the middle of giving herself a facial, there didn't seem much danger of it. Theo came, the earrings were safely smuggled back, together with the gold strappy sandals and the slinky dress (with the pins taken out and the hem untacked) and Laurel swore that from *here on in* (an expression she had picked up from Dad, who had picked it up in America) she was going to be a model of good behaviour.

"After all," she said, piously, "it's up to me to set an example to the rest of you."

"Well, get her!" jeered Rose.

For the whole of the following week, Laurel was quite unbearable. She censored their television – "You can't watch that! Mum wouldn't approve." "You've sat there for over two hours, that's quite long enough!"

She organised a cleaning rota – "It's your turn to do the dusting!" "It's your turn to polish the furniture!"

She started checking that their beds had been made and their bedrooms were tidy. She told Jazz off for not cleaning the bath – "You've been cutting your toenails in it. Ugh! Disgusting!" She raged at Rose for dropping crumbs over the sitting room carpet – "which I have just *vacuumed*". She even had a go at poor little innocent Daisy for not clearing up a fur ball that one of the cats had deposited on the upstairs landing.

"I didn't know it was there!" wept Daisy.

"Well, I don't know how you missed it! I saw it the minute I went up there. How do you think Mum's going to feel, coming home and treading in a fur ball?"

"Oh, stop it!" cried Jazz. "You're nothing but a *nag*!"

"A harridan," said Rose.

"I am just trying," said Laurel, "to keep a bit of order round here."

Rose stomped off, muttering about "power going to people's heads".

"It's for Mum!" shrieked Laurel. "Poor Mum," she added, virtuously. "She's working herself to a shadow. The least we can do," she yelled, "is try to make life a bit easier for her!"

Certainly the house was clean and tidy – a great deal cleaner and tidier than when Mum was around. Mum wasn't much use at housework. One thing she and Dad had always agreed on, a bit of a mess made a place look lived in. But Laurel wasn't having any of it. She harried them relentlessly.

"It will be so nice when Mum's back," sighed Daisy.

One day towards the end of Mum's second week of filming, Rose came home from school with her face all scrunched and scowling.

"What's the matter?" said Jazz. "You look like you've been up for the lead and been given an understudy!"

"Huh!" said Rose.

She sat in grim silence all through tea, then went off – still in silence – to her room.

"Something's happened," said Jazz. Rose was one of those people, a bit like Dad, who tended to clam up. Jazz and Laurel were more like Mum. Everyone knew when they were upset: they banged about and made a lot of noise. But it didn't take much for Jazz and Laurel to start banging. It took a great deal to upset Rose. She was what Dad called well-balanced.

"Daisy, go and see if you can find out," said Jazz. If Rose was going to confide in anyone, it would be Daisy. "Ask her what's wrong."

"All right." Daisy trotted off, obediently.

"And tell her it's her turn to do the washing-up!" bawled Laurel.

"Oh, don't fuss!" cried Jazz. "I'll do it for her!"

"*No*." Laurel stamped a foot. "She can't be allowed to get out of things just because she's in a hump. We all have to take our turn."

Really, thought Jazz, there were times when Laurel–in–love, however tiresome, was vastly to be preferred to Laurel–out–of–love. Laurel–out–of–love was just one big *pain*.

After a few minutes Daisy came trotting back downstairs with the news that a teacher at school had accused Rose of cheating.

"*Cheating?*" Jazz and Laurel echoed it, incredulously.

"He wouldn't give her a mark for her homework. He

said she must have copied it from somewhere."

"That's ridiculous!" Jazz threw down the dish mop. "Let me go and talk to her!"

Jazz went storming up to Rose's bedroom.

"Who is this teacher? What's he on about?"

The teacher was Mr Gallimore, who took them for English. He was new that term so Jazz didn't know him very well. Obviously, she thought, he didn't know Rose at all. Nobody who knew Rose would ever accuse her of cheating.

"Where is it?" said Jazz. "This thing he thinks you've copied?"

Silently, Rose handed over a wodge of paper. Eight pages! All covered in Rose's neat, square writing.

"What is it? An essay?"

Rose nodded.

"Where does he think you copied it from?"

Rose humped a shoulder. She had gone into her non-talking mode, which meant that she was really upset.

"Can I take it downstairs, to show Laurel?"

"If you want."

"I mean, *I* know you didn't copy it," said Jazz. "I just want to see why he thinks you might have done."

Rose looked at her, rather hard.

"I'm not doubting you," said Jazz. "But I've got to read it, haven't I?"

Rose said nothing, just very slowly turned away.

"You stay here. I'll be back," said Jazz. "We're not letting him get away with it!"

Downstairs, she spread the pages on the kitchen table. Laurel viewed them with alarm.

"How much has she written?"

"Eight pages," said Jazz.

"*Eight pages?*"

You know what she's like. I think we ought to read it."

Laurel pulled a face. "I'm not wading through all that lot!"

"Read it out to us," said Daisy.

"All right." Jazz never minded a bit of reading aloud. She cleared her throat. "*My View of Society*. That's what it's called. *Society is a conglomerate of individuals. Each—*"

"What's a kerglomrit?" said Daisy.

"Oh! Um – well, a sort of – mixture. *Each individual is a cog in the wheel of life—*"

"Oh, wow," said Laurel.

"*—but some cogs are more important than other cogs. A few cogs are extremely rich and powerful—*"

Laurel groaned. Daisy said, "What's she going on about cogs for?"

"Look," said Jazz, "am I reading this or not? 'Cos if I am, then just shut up and listen."

They listened, in awed silence, as Jazz worked her way through the whole eight pages. Every now and then she would stumble and have to go back to the beginning of a sentence to make sense of it. Sometimes she came across words that she didn't fully understand or wasn't quite sure how to pronounce. But that was Rose for you. It didn't mean she had copied them. She just naturally knew words that most people hadn't even heard of.

"Well?" Jazz shuffled the pages back into order.

"Is that it?" said Laurel, relieved.

"I didn't understand hardly any of it," said Daisy.

"It's all the stuff she reads. I can see *why* he thought she might have copied it—"

"But she didn't!" Jazz stated it, very fiercely.

"No, well, *we* know she didn't," said Laurel.

"She didn't! Rose doesn't do things like that. And look what the creep has written at the bottom! *I would have preferred to have your own ideas rather than someone else's.* Cheek!"

"He asked her where she'd got it from," said Daisy.

"What did she say?"

"She said she got it out of her head but he didn't believe her."

"So now he's accusing her of lying, as well! What are we going to do?" demanded Jazz.

"Don't see that we can do anything," said Laurel.

"We can't *prove* she got it out of her head."

"If she says she did, then she did! I'm going to have it out with him," declared Jazz.

"No, don't, you mustn't!" Laurel seized hold of her arm as if she thought Jazz might be going off to do battle right there and then. "Just leave things alone!"

"No way!" said Jazz. "I'm not having my sister called a cheat and a liar!"

"But you can't have a go at a teacher!"

"I won't have a go. I'll just tell him."

"You'll get all loud and obstreperous."

"I won't get loud and obstreperous! I shall keep calm as calm," said Jazz.

"Maybe we should wait till Mum comes home," said Daisy. "She could go and talk to him."

"*No*. Mum's got enough to do. I'm going to handle this," said Jazz.

Next day, last period before lunch, Jazz's class had English with Mr Gallimore. He was youngish – well, not positively ancient – and quite reasonable looking. In fact Jazz's friend Carmel had a bit of a thing about him. She thought he was gorgeous. But Carmel always went for the older man; she said boys were just too silly and boring. Her eyes grew round as soup plates when at the end of class Jazz hissed, "See you outside. I want to talk to Mr Gallimore."

"What about?" mouthed Carmel, but Jazz shook her head. She wouldn't even tell her best friend what Rose had been accused of.

"Yes, Jasmine?" said Mr Gallimore. "What can I do for you?"

Jazz stood with her hands clasped behind her, one in the other, very tightly. Last night, all fired up, she could hardly wait to go rushing into the fray. This morning, faced with the reality of Mr Gallimore actually sitting there, waiting for her to say something, she found herself not feeling quite so brave. But it had to be done!

"Well?" said Mr Gallimore. He smiled at her, encouragingly. He probably thought she had a question about the text they had been studying. He liked people to ask questions. "You have a problem?"

"It's not me," said Jazz. "It's my sister."

"And who is your sister?"

"Rose Jones."

"Oh!" He tipped his chair back, bracing his knees against the edge of the desk. "So Rose is your sister, is she?"

"Yes, and my sister doesn't cheat!" said Jazz.

Mr Gallimore raised an eyebrow. "I wasn't aware that anyone had accused her of doing so."

"You said she copied her essay off someone else!"

"And didn't she?"

"No, she did not!" Jazz could feel herself starting to shake. She clenched her hands even tighter. She had promised Laurel that she would stay calm! "You don't understand about Rose," she said. "She's like...well! She's really really clever."

"I grant you she's bright," said Mr Gallimore.

"She's not just bright, she's—"

Jazz floundered, unsure how to put it. You could hardly say your sister was some kind of genius.

Mr Gallimore said it for her.

"A genius?" he suggested. "Child prodigy, perhaps?"

Now he was being sarcastic. He wasn't taking her seriously! Jazz felt the anger welling up inside her. If only Dad had been here! Not Mum. Mum was too much like Jazz. Ruled by her emotions. Dad was more laid back. He would know how to keep his cool.

"That essay," said Mr Gallimore, "would have been a remarkable piece of work from a Year 10 pupil."

"Yes, because Rose is remarkable! And she doesn't cheat! She doesn't have to."

"No one ever said she was cheating." Mr Gallimore was starting to sound a trifle testy. "She's obviously been doing some pretty heavy reading – for which she is to be congratulated – and she's simply copied down what she's read. That's not cheating, that's—"

"A lie!" cried Jazz. "Rose doesn't *copy* things. She

115

reads things and she thinks about them and then she makes up her own mind. And then she writes them down in her own words!"

"Yes," said Mr Gallimore, "and very extraordinary some of them are, too! I doubt, if I asked her, she'd even know what they meant."

"Of course she would!" Jazz was scornful. "She never uses words she doesn't understand. She has a very wide vocabulary. I bet if she was white and spoke all posh" – Jazz put on her actress voice – "I bet then you wouldn't say she'd copied it! You just have low expectations on account of she's black!"

There was a moment of appalled silence. Jazz trembled from head to foot. How could she have said such a thing? To a *teacher*? It was the sort of argument that Rose herself might use – and they would all groan and go, "Don't start!"

"I'm s–sorry," stammered Jazz. Now she'd blown it. She'd be put on report for sure. Laurel had said she would start yelling, but not even Laurel had thought she'd go that far. Accusing a teacher of racism!

Jazz swallowed. "I d–didn't mean—"

Mr Gallimore brought his chair back to earth with a bang.

"Don't apologise! You spoke your mind, you said what you thought. It happens to be wrong, but… it's a valid point. Sometimes we do have expectations that are too low. I'll look again at Rose's essay; we'll have a chat about it. I may have misjudged her."

I can't believe I'm hearing this, thought Jazz.

"Thank you," she whispered.

"No, thank you for bringing it to my attention." said Mr Gallimore.

Jazz went reeling out into the yard. Carmel ran up to her.

"What happened? What were you talking about?"

"Oh—" Jazz waved a hand. "This and that."

"You mean, you're not going to tell me?"

"I can't," said Jazz. "It was about Rose. But he's all right, Mr Gallimore!"

"Could have told you that," said Carmel.

seven

LITTLE WOMEN HAD finished. It was now going off on a three-month tour, all up and down the country, but Mum was not going with it.

"My touring days are over," she said. "Too much like hard work!"

"But it would be *money*," said Rose.

"Yes, and you wouldn't see anything of me! Is that what you want?"

"No!" Daisy hurled herself at Mum, clutching her

tight with both hands, as if Mum might be going to set off right that very moment for the Outer Hebrides.

"We all have to make sacrifices," said Rose.

"Mum, no!" Daisy tightened her grip. "Please, Mum!"

"It's all right, sweety pie!" Mum pulled Daisy on to her lap. Most people, at twelve, were too old for cuddles, but not Daisy. "I've already told them I'm not going. I'm staying here, to be with you."

"But the bills!" wailed Rose. Two had come plopping through the letter box only that morning. Nasty ones. Red ones. "How are we going to pay the bills?"

"We'll find a way," said Mum. "Something will turn up!"

Mum and Dad had been saying that for as long as Jazz could remember. It was all part and parcel of being an actor. You never knew where your next job was going to come from – but something would turn up.

"Would you have gone on tour if Dad had been here?" she said.

Mum scrunched her lips, the way she always did when anyone mentioned Dad.

"That's irrelevant!" she snapped. "He isn't here, so the question doesn't arise."

You couldn't ever talk to Mum about Dad. Jazz couldn't decide whether it was because she was still too cross or whether it was because it upset her. She never wanted to speak to him when he rang; she never asked how he was or what he was up to. But Jazz had noticed that she always hung about and listened when the rest of them were swopping information. She always pretended that she wasn't, like she would suddenly become very busy plumping up the sofa cushions or searching for something in a kitchen drawer; but Jazz could tell that she was taking it all in.

"It's so nice having Mum at home," sighed Daisy. "I wish she could be at home all the time!"

"You mean, never do any more acting?" said Jazz, shocked.

"Just be an ordinary mum," pleaded Daisy.

"*Bor*-ring!" Jazz and Laurel chanted it together, but Daisy shook her head. She could be quite stubborn, in her own quiet way.

"I think it would be lovely."

"Yes, until the bills came in," said Rose. "Then we wouldn't be able to pay *anything* and we'd all end up in a bed-and-breakfast."

Rose, just recently, had become obsessed by bills. Every time a new one dropped on to the mat she'd carry it through to the kitchen and in the voice of doom announce, "*Another one*."

To begin with, Mum tried making a joke of it. She

120

stuck all the bills round the large mirror in the sitting room, as if they were telegrams.

"Look, there's a red one! Isn't it pretty?"

But after a while, even Mum started worrying. Jazz knew things must be bad when one afternoon, at tea time, she said that if nothing turned up she might seriously have to consider looking for a proper job.

There was a startled silence.

"But what could you do?" faltered Laurel. "There isn't anything you could do!"

"I'm not that useless," said Mum. "There must be something I could do?"

"Like what?"

"Well, I could – I could work in a shop! I could work in an office."

"No, you couldn't," said Rose. "You don't know how to use a computer."

"I could learn! Maybe I ought to enrol for evening classes. I could be someone's secretary!" Mum put on her reading glasses and sat up straight on her chair, wearing a suitable secretary expression, demure and rather prim. She smiled round the table. "How's that?"

"It's not you!" Jazz said it earnestly. She couldn't imagine Mum in an office. Mum was a free spirit! She was an *actress*. She couldn't be chained to a desk and a computer!

"Well, I've got to do something," said Mum. "We can't go on like this!"

"I feel so guilty," confessed Laurel later that day to Jazz. "It doesn't seem right I should be so happy when Mum's so worried!"

Laurel was over the moon because she had been chosen to model clothes in a fashion show. The show was being run by a local store, with all the proceeds to go to charity. Parents had been invited to submit photographs of their children, so Laurel had submitted one of herself, without telling Mum, and that very morning she had received a letter inviting her to take part.

"It's the start of my career!" she said excitedly.

Rose had wanted to know if she was going to be paid.

"Certainly not," said Laurel, indignant. "It's for charity."

"That's a pity," said Rose. "It would have come in handy for the gas bill."

"Oh, Rose, don't!" begged Mum. "Something will turn up!"

That was before she had decided she would have to go out and get a proper job. But how could she? thought Jazz. What would happen if Mum were working in someone's office and the telephone suddenly rang and it was her agent asking her to go for an audition? She couldn't not go! It might be her big chance! If you were an actor you had to be prepared to seize every opportunity. They couldn't let Mum go out and get a proper job!

She called the others to a conference.

"What are we going to do?"

"Don't see what we can do," said Rose.

"Well, we can't just sit back and twiddle our thumbs!"

"Maybe," said Laurel, "we could—"

"What?" They turned on her, hopefully.

"Maybe we could… sell something?"

Jazz pulled a face. "Sell what? We haven't got anything!"

"We must have *something*."

"Let's all go away and make a list," said Daisy.

Their lists didn't amount to very much. Jazz, who wasn't really a jewellery kind of person, had put down the gold Maltese cross that Nan had given her for her twelfth birthday. Laurel, who had also had a Maltese cross, had put down a glass paperweight with a snowstorm inside it, a present from Lady Jayne. She hadn't mentioned the Maltese cross.

"I'm not selling that!" she said, when Jazz asked why she hadn't included it. "It's my only piece of jewellery!"

Rose had put down her Swiss cuckoo clock, which she said was tacky and twee.

"That won't fetch much," said Jazz. "The cuckoo's broken. What about your personal organiser? That might be worth something."

"But I need it!" Rose's organiser was the nearest thing she had to a computer. "What about your copy of that play?"

"*Much Ado?* I'm not parting with that!" cried Jazz. "It's signed by Laurence Olivier!"

"So it could be worth money," said Laurel.

"Well, and so could your Maltese cross! But you won't put it on the list."

Daisy was the only one who was prepared to make real sacrifices. She had included three of her most treasured possessions: a music box, with a ballerina who turned in circles as the music played; a Victorian doll that had belonged to Nan's nan; and a real Spanish fan that Dad had brought back from Spain.

"Daisy!" Jazz looked at her, aghast. "You can't sell those! You love them!"

Daisy's lip quivered. "I just thought it might help."

"Now I suppose you'll expect me to sell my organiser," said Rose, crossly.

There was a pause. Jazz thought of her signed copy of *Much Ado*; Laurel, no doubt, of her Maltese cross.

"Oh, look, this is ridiculous!" cried Rose. "Even if we sold everything we had, it still wouldn't pay all the bills. And even if it did, what are we supposed to do next time?"

With guilty relief, Jazz mentally put *Much Ado* back in its special case and turned the key.

"So what's the solution?" she said.

"There isn't one. Either Mum gives up acting and gets a proper job *or* something turns up *or* we go bankrupt and have to live on the streets. I can't worry about it any more," declared Rose.

The very next day, something wonderful happened. Something turned up – but for Jazz, not for Mum. Jazz couldn't believe it when Theo rang to tell her the news.

"Dad wants to use you in his next telly production."

"*Me?*" gasped Jazz. "He wants to use *me?*"

"It's only a couple of lines," warned Theo. "Nothing to get excited about."

But Jazz would have got excited if it hadn't been any lines at all! Just the chance to be on television…

"I told him I wouldn't be in it unless he used you," said Theo. "I told him I'm sick of being an actor but that it's what you want to do more than anything in the world, so he said OK, he said it would be good to have someone from an ethnic minority."

Is that what I am? wondered Jazz. Someone from an

ethnic minority? But she was too thrilled to niggle about it.

"You'll get paid, of course," said Theo.

Paid??? She would have done it for nothing!

"It's three days' work 'cos we're in other scenes where we don't have to say anything, so it'll probably be about... couple of hundred."

"*Pounds?*" gasped Jazz.

"Well, or two-fifty. Maybe three. I know it's not very much, but I hope you'll do it. For my sake," urged Theo. "You've got to!"

"I will," Jazz assured him. Let them try to stop her!

"Dad says does your mum want him to go through her agent, and to tell her it's in the Easter holidays so you won't have to miss any school?"

"I'll tell her!"

Jazz went racing off there and then to deliver the news.

"Mum, Mum, I'm going to be on telly!"

A babble of questions broke out.

"When?"

"Who for?"

"What in?"

"Easter holidays, for Theo's dad! I don't know what in... I forgot to ask!"

"Will you be paid?" said Rose.

Jazz nodded, ecstatically. "£200! Maybe more."

Two hundred pounds would bring her drama school fund to a quite dizzying amount. Maybe enough for her to pay the first term's fees...

She found that Rose was tugging at her sleeve.

"*Bills*," mouthed Rose.

Jazz's heart went clunk! into her shoes. Was Rose really hinting that she should use her first ever acting money to pay the gas bill? The electricity bill? The telephone bill?

I won't! she thought. It's not fair!

Mum held out her arms. "Come here, and let me congratulate you... my little actress! You know I don't think it's at all a sensible career, in fact I'm dead against it, but—" She threw up her hands. "What can I do? I didn't take my mum's advice, I don't expect you'll take mine."

"No, I won't," said Jazz, grinning.

Rose shook her head. "It'll all lead to gloom and despair. Out on the street, living in a box."

"Oh, Rose, hush!" said Mum. "Don't ruin it for her."

"*Well.*" Rose stared at Jazz; a horridly penetrating stare.

Oh, bother! thought Jazz. Damn and bother and *blast*. Damnation and *hell*. She took a breath.

"When I get paid," she said. Damn damn *damn*. "We could use it for some of the bills."

"What?" Mum's eyebrows shot up into her hair. "I'm not using my daughter's hard-earned money for paying bills! That will be *your* money; you hang on to it. Don't worry about the bills, something will turn up. Something," said Mum, "always does."

"And sure enough, something did. It wasn't what they were expecting – but that just made it even better.

On Friday afternoon, just as they got in from school, Dad rang. It was Jazz who answered the phone.

"Guess what?" said Dad. "Guess where I'm calling from?"

Dad was calling from England!

"Just the other side of town, baby. How 'bout we all meet up for the weekend and I take you some place nice?"

"Mum as well?" said Jazz.

Dad hesitated. "Would she come, do you think?"

"I – don't know. I could ask her!"

But Mum wouldn't. "Why should I want to see him?" she said. "What's he doing over here, anyway?"

"He wouldn't tell me. He's going to tell us tomorrow. He's taking us out for a meal!"

"Hm! Someone obviously has money to burn. You might ask him, if he's come into a fortune, to channel some of it this way. Just remind him," said Mum, "that he does have four growing girls to provide for." Jazz sighed. This would be the first time they had seen Dad in almost a year. She didn't want to nag him! But Rose said Mum was quite right.

"Men can't expect to have children and then run off and not take their share of the responsibility."

"Oh, shut up being so politically correct!"

"I'm not being politically correct," said Rose. "You just shut up being sexist! Why's it always left to the women?"

"Look, you two, we don't want to fight," said Laurel.

"Let's just concentrate on being happy!"

"Well, we have to mention it," hissed Rose.

"We *will*," said Jazz, "but not right at the start! And anyway, it hasn't all been left to Mum. What about some of the cheques that came in? They were Dad's!"

"I know. I was just *saying*."

"Don't!" Laurel clapped her hands over her ears. "I don't want to hear another word! Not from either of you!"

Dad came to pick them up after breakfast next day. Daisy was so excited at the thought of seeing him again she could hardly keep still and kept racing from room to room, from window to window. Even Mum, who refused to come to the door to say hello – "What do I want to speak to him for?" – couldn't resist the occasional peek from behind the sitting room curtains.

"There he is!" yelled Laurel, at last.

Daisy gave a great squeal and went rushing out into the hall. Mum sniffed.

"All this big build up! I just hope it doesn't end in tears." Jazz looked at Mum, reproachfully.

"Oh, sweetheart, I'm sorry!" Mum flew at Jazz and hugged her. "He's your dad, of course you're excited! Don't take any notice of me, I'm just a sour old woman. Off you go!" She gave Jazz a little push. "Have a good day."

"Are you sure you don't want to come and say hello?"

Just for a moment, she thought Mum might be weakening; but then they heard Daisy's joyous cry of "*Dad!*" and Mum's lips went into their tightening routine.

"No, thank you," she said. "I don't think so."

"But, Mum!"

"Maybe next time," said Mum.

Jazz turned, and walked, rather slowly, across the room. She found herself strangely nervous at the prospect of being with Dad again. It was so long since they had seen him! Would he be the same Dad that she remembered?

She went through to the hall – and there he was, the same old Dad! Jazz caught her breath and stood, suddenly shy, in the doorway. Dad held out his arms.

"Hi, baby!"

Her cheeks fired up. She had forgotten how handsome he was, her dad. "Drop dead gorgeous!" She had laughed when Carmel, one time, had said that. But it was true! It was true! Dad really was tall, dark and handsome. Like a film star!

"Well?" He laughed. "Are you just going stand there?"

"No!"

Jazz hurled herself at him. For just a moment she had been scared that she might be tongue-tied – Jazz, who was never at a loss for words! But no one could be tongue-tied with Dad for very long. By the time he had swept them off their feet, one after another – even Rose, who liked to stand on her dignity: even Laurel, who considered herself grown up – they were all clamouring for the opportunity to get in first with their bits of news.

"Dad, guess what? I'm going to be on telly!"

"Dad, I'm going to be in a fashion show!"

"Dad, Tink got lost! But I found him again!" That was Daisy, very proud.

"*I* got an A+ for one of my essays." Rose; who else?

"So what do you all want?" laughed Dad. "Gold stars?"

"No! We want to hear about *you*," said Laurel.

"All in good time, baby! All in good time."

They set off up the road, Daisy on one side of Dad, clutching his hand, Jazz on the other, Rose and Laurel in front.

"I take it your mum didn't want to come and say hello to me?"

"She said maybe next time," said Jazz.

"She still not happy with me?"

"We–e–e–ll…" Jazz hunched a shoulder.

"Just as well I didn't ask if we could use the car. I get the feeling she might have said no."

"We don't need the car!" Rose danced jubilantly ahead of them up the road. "Cars are stinky!"

"Quite right," said Dad. "Let's all jump on a bus!"

Getting on a bus with Dad was almost a treat in itself. They took the number 88 all the way to Trafalgar Square and went to have coffee and cakes in the restaurant of the National Gallery. Well, Dad had coffee, and so did Laurel, trying to be grown up; the others had Cokes. But they all had wondrous sticky buns of the type that Mum didn't very often let them eat.

"Full of calories! Ugh! *Bad*," said Jazz, in Mum's voice.

"Now, don't go and tell on me," said Dad. "I'm in quite enough hot water as it is."

At this point, Rose dug Jazz very hard in the ribs.

Jazz squirmed. She knew Rose wanted her to bring up the subject of bills. But not now! she thought. Not while we're having fun.

"Do you want me to let you into a secret?" said Dad. Daisy nodded, blissfully.

"I been back in England since just before Christmas."

Just before *Christmas*? That was almost four months ago!

"Why didn't you tell us?" whispered Jazz.

"I felt so bad," said Dad. "No job, no money… just a useless bum. I didn't know how to face you. It's what this business does to a person. It can really bring you to your knees. Know what I'm saying?"

Jazz nodded, solemnly. It was what Lady Jayne was forever telling them.

"And then – wham!" Dad broke into a beam. The old, happy, Dad-beam that they knew so well. "My luck turned!"

"How?" Jazz leaned forward eagerly; but Dad shook his head.

"I can't tell you! Not right now. It's a secret."

"*Dad!*"

Dad put a finger to his mouth. "My lips are sealed, baby… much as my life is worth. Tell me about your mum! How are you all coping?"

"Um – well." Jazz crinkled her brow.

"We're not," said Rose, bluntly. "Mum's show's finished and she's waiting for something else to turn up and while she's waiting we've got so many bills she says we could paper a room with them."

"Rose," said Laurel, "it's not that bad!"

"Yes, it is," said Rose. "Mum's dead worried. She's even talking of going out and getting a proper job."

"Hey, hey, we can't have that! No way!" Dad suddenly put a hand in his jacket pocket and brought out an envelope. He slid it across the table to Rose. "You give her this. Tell her there'll be more. Tell her just to hang on in there. OK?"

"What is it?" said Rose.

Laurel snatched at it. "It's for Mum! Nothing to do with you."

They were all sad when the time came for Dad to take them home. Daisy wept, and clung to him.

"I don't want you to go! I want you to come back and live with us again!"

"Oh, baby!" Dad held her to him. "I wish it could be. But your mum—" He glanced at the others, over Daisy's head. "I don't reckon your mum would be too agreeable to that idea?"

There was a silence. Jazz chewed her lip, Laurel

stared at the ground. Only Rose was brave enough to say anything.

"She's still really mad."

"Yeah." Dad nodded. "I guess I gave her cause."

"It wasn't all you!" Jazz burst out with it. "It was both of you!"

"That's my baby!" Dad reached out a hand and ran it over Jazz's cropped head. "You stick up for your old dad."

"Not old," muttered Jazz.

"I'm not sticking up for either of you," said Rose. "I think grown-ups are pathetic, if you want to know. Utterly *pathetic*." And Rose went marching off, up the path, slamming the gate behind her.

Dad sighed, and unwrapped Daisy's arms from round his waist.

"I've got to let you go, baby. But I'll be back!"

"W–when?" stammered Daisy.

"Soon! I'll be back soon."

"Are you going off somewhere?" said Jazz. "Are you *filming*?"

Dad tapped the side of his nose.

"Why can't you tell us?"

" 'Cos I've taken an oath!"

"But when are we going to see you?" screeched Daisy.

"I'll make you a promise," said Dad. "Beginning of May… my sacred, solemnest word! That's not too long to wait, now, is it?"

They speculated all evening on what Dad could have meant. Mum speculated along with the rest of them.

"Something's turned up, that's for sure… I knew he was back! I knew he couldn't be calling from the States! You remember?" She turned to Jazz. "You remember, at Christmas? I tried dialling 1471? But all I got was *Caller withheld their number.* Honestly! That man!"

"He was ashamed," said Jazz.

"Ashamed of what? Being out of work? So what's new? We're all out of work! And now he's got something and he won't tell you. Why not?"

"He's taken an oath."

"Oh, rubbish!" said Mum. "He's just enjoying himself, keeping us in the dark."

"Well, at any rate we can pay the bills," said Rose. In the envelope that Dad had given them was a cheque for a sum which had momentarily stunned even Mum into silence. "At least we shan't have to go and live in a box. And he *said*," said Rose, "that there'd be more."

"Oh, don't be so money-grubbing all the time!" cried Jazz.

"I'm not being."

"Yes, you are! Always on about *bills*."

136

"Bills," said Rose, crushingly, "have to be paid."

"Unfortunately," agreed Mum, "Rose is right. I'm just glad your dad showed a proper sense of responsibility."

"He did it by himself." Jazz was quick to point it out.

"He'd got the cheque already written! We didn't have to ask him."

All Mum said to that was, "Humph!"

We're really going to have to work on her, thought Jazz. There had to be a way to get Mum and Dad back together!

eight

"OH. WHY DO you girls have to be so *fractious* all the time?" cried Mum, one morning at breakfast.

"What's frackshus?" Daisy wanted to know.

"Bickering and backbiting and totally ungrateful!"

It was true they had been rather quarrelsome of late. Jazz and Laurel had quarrelled on the subject of clothes. Jazz had accused Laurel of dolling herself up just to please men, while Laurel had accused Jazz of slobbing around like a refugee from Oxfam. No man, she said, would ever look twice at her.

"Don't want them to!" had declared Jazz.

Laurel had said in that case she would end up as a sour and embittered old maid; to which Jazz had retorted, "And a good thing, too! At least it's better than being some empty-headed bimbo!"

Rose had sided with Jazz on that occasion; but then she had started lecturing Laurel about "only going out with white boys. First it was that creep Simon, now it's that creep from Year 12."

"Martin Balcombe! He's not a creep."

"He's white," said Rose.

"So what?"

"So why can't you go out with a black boy? If you've *got* to go out with boys."

"Yes, I have, and why should I?" screeched Laurel, getting herself in a muddle. "What business is it of yours, anyway?"

Jazz sided with Laurel on that one. Rose really could be quite impossible! But even Daisy seemed to have caught the bug. Peevishly she demanded to know who had shut poor Tink in the airing cupboard.

"He's been there for hours! He could have *suffocated*. You'd think people could just *look* before they close the door!"

"Well, it wasn't me," said Jazz.

"Wasn't me," said Laurel.

"Wasn't me," said Rose.

"It had to be someone!" shrieked Daisy. "Poor little thing! He couldn't close the door by himself, could he?"

"What's the matter with you all?" said Mum. "Haven't enough good things been happening?"

Good things *had* happened. For all of them. Mum's good thing was that *Icing* had been scheduled for repeats. That meant loads of money. It also meant that Mum's face would be back on television, and who knew where that might lead?

Laurel's good thing was that she had done her fashion show and had her picture in the paper. Mum had bought a copy of the original print and had it blown up, and now it was in a frame, on the sitting room wall. Laurel could be seen taking surreptitious peeks at it when she thought no one was watching her.

Jazz had done her television part and had lived in a state of high excitement from beginning to end. Theo might keep yawning and complaining that "It's all so *boring*!" but to Jazz a television studio was like an Aladdin's cave, full of wonder and delight. She couldn't wait to do more! And Theo's dad, the great Rufus White, had promised her that she would.

"Now that I've seen what you can do, I shall certainly bear you in mind!"

Jazz had been so thrilled she couldn't stop repeating the words, over and over, in her head: *I shall bear you in mind, I shall bear you in mind...* And next time, perhaps, he might trust her with a real part!

"I don't mean to be greedy, she thought, but it would be lovely to have more lines!

And after all, you had to aim high if you wanted to get anywhere. Jazz didn't intend to turn into another Lady Jayne. She was going to be a STAR!

Rose, in her own way, was already a star. Her end-of-term report had made her sound, said Laurel, without any trace of envy, like some kind of child genius. Which of course she was! The family had long known it. But it was nice that other people had found out. The only subjects where she wasn't a genius were PE – *Rose does not exert herself*, Home Economics – *Rose shows no aptitude*, and Handicrafts – *Rose appears to lack coordination*. For English, Mr Gallimore had written: *Rose is a quite exceptional student. Her written work betrays an understanding and grasp of language far beyond her years.*

Jazz glowed when she read that. Rose just shrugged and made like she couldn't have cared less, but Jazz still remembered the day she had come home from school upset because Mr Gallimore had accused her of cheating. Rose knew that she was bright; she didn't need people to tell her so. But she was human, the same as the rest of them! Jazz bet she had stolen just as many surreptitious peeks at her report as Laurel had at her photograph.

As for Daisy, she had perhaps had the biggest triumph of them all, for Daisy had actually been awarded her school prize for Student who has Tried Hardest, and what was more, she had gone up on stage, in front of three hundred people, to receive it! A year ago, wild horses wouldn't have dragged Daisy on stage.

I knew we were right to send her to Linden Hyrst," said Mum. "If only that stupid man had been there! He'd have been so proud! Well, it's his own fault. I don't see why I should shed any tears over it."

But at least she had mentioned him! And Jazz couldn't help noticing that Dad had progressed from being *that man* to that *stupid* man. As if maybe Mum felt just a little regretful. She exchanged glances with Laurel. Was Mum softening?

She certainly wasn't softening that morning at breakfast.

"I'm sick of the lot of you!" she said. "You do nothing but whimper and whinge."

"I was only *saying*," said Rose, aggrieved, "it's all very well spending all this money on drama school—"

"It's my money!" shouted Jazz. "I earnt it!"

"But you're so *unaware*," said Rose. "Get real! How many black actresses ever earn a living?"

"How many *actresses* ever earn a living?" said Mum. "I've already been through all this with her! My mum went through it with me. I didn't take any notice; why should Jazz?"

Jazz looked at her mum, gratefully.

"I'm just trying to make her aware," sighed Rose. "I don't want it to come as a rude shock."

"I am aware, thank you very much," said Jazz. You couldn't be brought up in a theatrical family and not be.

"It's a sexist world out there."

"Not just sexist! *Racist*. It's even worse for black actresses than white."

Laurel groaned; long and deeply.

"Why do you keep on about being black all the time?" said Jazz, irritably. "We're not black, we're half and half!"

"That's right," said Mum, who could rarely resist the chance to join in an argument. "Are you trying to deny part of your heritage?"

"No, I'm facing facts," said Rose. "And anyway, it's a political statement."

Jazz tossed her head. "You can be a political statement if you like! I'd rather just be a human being."

"Well, you can't," said Rose. "It's not the way people see you."

"It's the way *I* see me."

"That's what I'm saying! You're not being realistic. You only got that telly part 'cos of Theo's dad thinking it would be good to have someone from an ethnic minority."

There was a silence.

"I don't think that's very kind," said Mum.

"But it's true! She told me. It's *tokenism*," said Rose. "So long as you have just one person from an ethnic minority, they can't accuse you of being racist. That's all they do it for."

"Oh, shut up!" cried Jazz. "Just *shut up*!"

Jazz pushed back her chair and blundered from the room. Trust Rose! Why did she always, *always* have to go and ruin things?

Later, Mum came upstairs to give Jazz a hug.

"Rose doesn't mean to be hurtful. You have to remember, no matter how clever she is, she's still only eleven years old. She still sees things very much in – well!" Mum laughed. "Black and white."

"She's right, though, isn't she?" Jazz scrubbed at her eyes. "They'll never let me play Beatrice, or Ophelia, or – or anything in Shakespeare!"

"How do you know?" said Mum. "Things are getting better. People are beginning to fight for their rights... gay people. Disabled people. Black people. *Women!* Rose is right about one thing, we do have to face up to reality, but that doesn't mean being defeatist."

"But Theo's dad did say it would be good to have someone from an ethnic m–minority!"

"Well, maybe he did, but he wouldn't have used you if he didn't think you could do it. And he certainly wouldn't have said he'd like to use you again! You obviously made an impression on him. So cheer up! And don't let Rose get to you. She still has to learn a bit of discretion."

Jazz didn't personally think that Rose would ever learn discretion. She had visions of one day being a famous actress – because she *was* going to be – and of Rose putting her to shame by screaming and shouting and waving banners outside the theatre. And everyone would know that they were sisters and they would expect Jazz to scream and shout and wave banners. But I won't! thought Jazz. I don't care about all that. I just want to get on with my life!

She said this to Mum, and Mum said she knew exactly how Jazz felt.

The world needs people like Rose… people who are prepared to make a stand. But they're certainly not easy to live with!"

Dad had rung three times since that Saturday they had all gone out together. But he wouldn't ever say where he was ringing from! Jazz had tried pressing 1471, only to hear the recorded voice at the other end tonelessly informing her that "We do not have the caller's number." And whenever they tried ringing him at his flat on the other side of London, there was no reply.

"He's just playing games with us!" said Mum. "There's no reason for all this cloak and dagger stuff."

Meanwhile, Easter had come and gone, and so had the Easter holidays. They had started back at school, and any day now it would be the beginning of May – which was when Dad had promised they would see him again. Daisy had ringed it on the calendar in red pen. D. A. D., she had written.

"I'll murder him if he lets her down!" said Mum.

"Dad's not a let-down merchant," protested Jazz; but it was worrying, all the same. The disappointment would be hard to bear, and so would Mum's unspoken "I told you so."

And then one morning the newspapers were delivered – Mum's *Guardian* and the *Radio Times*. It was Daisy who ran to the door to collect them. The others were in the kitchen, eating breakfast, when they heard her high-pitched scream.

"My God!" cried Mum, shoving back her chair. "What's happened?"

"Mu–u–u–u–m!" Daisy practically fell into the kitchen.

146

She was waving the *Radio Times* above her head.

"What is it, what is it? Calm down!" shrieked Mum.

"Dad," whispered Daisy.

"*What?*"

Laurel snatched at the *Radio Times*. Her jaw fell open.

"Where, where? Let's see!" Jazz and Rose jostled to look over Laurel's shoulder.

"Hey! Wow!" Jazz jumped up and punched the air. "He's made it, he's made it!"

From the cover of the *Radio Times*, Dad's face grinned up at them. He was wearing a green uniform with gold piping. Underneath were the words, *New boy on the block. Actor T.J. Jones joins the Greens as Det. Insp. Ben Arlott.*

"*Green Force!*" Laurel waved the *Radio Times* at Mum. "He's got into *Green Force!*"

Green Force was the big one. One of the most successful series on television.

"It even sells to America," gloated Jazz.

Mum sniffed. "I still don't see the need for all that cloak and dagger stuff."

"Mum, it was a secret! It says—" Laurel had opened up the paper and had found the article inside. "It says, *TV's best kept secret.*"

"He probably had to sign something," said Rose.

"What else does it say?" Jazz craned to see. "Does it mention us? Ooh, yes, it does! It says he's got four daughters and is married to actress Debbie Silver, famous as best friend Sophie from *Icing on the Cake*. Isn't that nice?" Jazz beamed hopefully at Mum. "He talked about you!"

"Charmed, I'm sure," said Mum. "When is it on?"

"Tuesday."

"I suppose we'll have to watch." Mum said it grudgingly – but she said it. Jazz flashed a victorious glance at Laurel. Getting there!

At school, suddenly, they were famous again. They had been famous when Mum was in *Icing*, but that had been almost a year ago and Mum hadn't done a great deal of telly since then. It was nice to be famous, thought Jazz. She enjoyed it when people came up to her – even members of staff! – and said, "Is that your dad on the cover of *Radio Times*?" One day it was going to be her! But for the moment she was quite happy to bask in Dad's reflected glory.

"Now we know why he's never at home," said Laurel. "He's obviously been on location."

"I said he was off filming!" exulted Jazz.

On Tuesday evening they all gathered round the television, even Rose, who usually claimed she had better things to do.

"I feel all shivery," said Daisy. "I'm scared in case he forgets his lines!"

Nobody scoffed and pointed out that it was all on film. They were feeling a bit shivery themselves, wanting so much for Dad to be good.

"It all depends how they edit it," worried Jazz, "and whether he gets any close-ups."

"Sh!" said Rose. "It's starting!"

The opening credits showed Dad and the other members of *Green Force* going through their paces – an elite squad who travelled the world in pursuit of eco criminals. The first episode was about the dumping of toxic waste, which pleased serious-minded Rose.

"I'm glad he's doing something *sensible*."

"Not like my piece of frivolity," said Mum.

Laurel poked Rose in the ribs and frowned at her. Rose squirmed.

"I was only s—"

"*Quiet!*" roared Jazz.

After the first few minutes, they all started to relax. By the end, they were so absorbed in the story they had almost forgotten it was Dad they were watching.

"Was he all right?" Daisy turned anxiously to Mum for reassurance, but it was Jazz who answered.

"He was brilliant! And loads of close-ups. The camera really loves him! Not even *she*" – she jerked her thumb at Rose – "can say it was tokenism."

"N–no. It may have started off that way," said Rose.

"Someone high up probably said they ought to have at least one person from an ethnic minority. But at least it was a proper part."

"Proper part?" Laurel said it indignantly. "It was one of the leads! And where's Mum gone?"

"She just suddenly went," said Daisy.

Jazz and Laurel looked at each other.

"I hope she's not feeling left out."

"Why should she feel left out?"

"Well, because of Dad suddenly being a big star."

"But Mum's been a big star!"

"Not in anything as big as *Green Force*."

"No." Laurel bit her lip. "But Mum's always said she puts family before stardom!"

"Daisy, go and see where she is," said Jazz.

Daisy went off, coming back with the news that Mum was "Upstairs in her bedroom… I think she's crying."

"*Crying?*"

"That's w–what it sounded like."

"Go and find out why!"

Daisy, ever obedient, trotted off again.

"Well?" said Jazz, when she trotted back.

"All she said was, *That stupid man* and *Why do I still love the b*—" Daisy clapped a hand to her mouth. "I'm not allowed to say that word!"

"Doesn't matter," said Jazz. "You've told us what we want to know. She does still love him!"

"But if she loves him," said Daisy, "why does she call him that word I'm not allowed to say?"

" 'Cos she's mad at him."

"But she still loves him?"

"Yes! Which means," said Jazz, "that it's up to us to do something about it. Let's have a consultation!"

Mum came down just as they had finished consulting.

"What's going on?" she said. "Why are you all looking so guilty?"

"We're planning a coup," said Rose.

"And I'm going up to the attic to put it into operation," said Jazz.

Jazz sat, hunched over the ancient typewriter, doing her best to type without making any mistakes. She was typing the letter they had agreed on.

```
Dear Mr Jones,
  We have just witnessed your ace
performance in Green Force.
  As a result of this, we have
formed an official fan club.
  We would be very pleased if you
would attend a reception in your
honour this coming Saturday at
```

6 o'clock at the above address. (If
you are not away filming, that is.)
   Please respond!
   With love from the
   T.J. Jones Family Fan Club.

They sent the letter by first class post the following day, to Dad's flat. Jazz had steeled herself for disappointment – "He might not be here," she warned Daisy – but on Thursday evening the telephone rang. Jazz led the charge out into the hall. The others hovered at her elbow.

"Hi, there! This is T.J. Jones," said Dad's voice. "Responding as requested."

"Dad! Are you going to come?"

At the other end of the line, Jazz could hear Dad hesitate.

"Baby, you sure about this?" he said.

"Yes! We had a consultation. You've got to come!"

"But what about your mum?"

"We'll handle Mum. Dad, please! Be brave!"

It seemed silly telling Dad to be brave, when just yesterday evening they had watched him tackling hardened criminals without turning so much as a hair. But Dad laughed, rather ruefully, and said, "Well, just make sure there aren't any rolling pins or saucepans lying about."

Jazz promised that they would.

On Saturday evening, Laurel said to Mum, "We've got a surprise planned! You've got to dress up for it. So would you please go and put on something nice?"

"Why?" said Mum. "What's going on?"

"You'll find out," said Laurel. "It's a surprise!"

"Will I like it?"

There was a pause.

"We're hoping that you will," said Jazz.

The last few minutes, as they waited for Dad to arrive, were filled with apprehension. Mum sat sipping a Martini and looking grim and tense, as if she suspected. Daisy was glued to the window.

"I know what you're up to," said Mum. "I know you mean it for the best. But—"

At that moment, Daisy went spinning out into the hall, and the doorbell rang.

"You stay there," Laurel told Mum.

"Remember what we planned," hissed Jazz.

They had agreed that the minute Dad walked through the door, they would push him into the sitting room with Mum and leave the two of them together.

"No huggy-huggy kissy-kissy smoochy stuff… he goes *straight in*."

Dad seemed a bit alarmed to be bundled so unceremoniously into the sitting room. You would never have thought this was the man who had single-handedly fought against some of the most vicious criminals on earth. He looked, thought Jazz, trying not to giggle, more like Daniel being thrown into the lions' den…

"It's all right," she assured him. "We've locked all the saucepans away!"

Laurel slammed the sitting room door, grabbed hold of Daisy, and they all four went stampeding up the stairs and into Laurel's bedroom.

"How long shall we give them?" said Rose.

"Mm… half an hour?"

"Unless they start yelling."

If Mum and Dad started yelling, they would know that they had failed.

They sat on Laurel's bed, ears strained for the slightest sound. Half an hour had never passed so slowly, not even in a maths class. Laurel had set her alarm clock, and when it finally went off it frightened them almost out of their skins.

"That's it!" said Jazz. "Let's go!"

They crept downstairs and tiptoed up to the sitting room door. Silence! Laurel opened the door, just a crack.

"Can we come in?"

Mum and Dad sprang apart, like two naughty children.

"My fan club!" said Dad.

Mum went to sit demurely on the sofa, doing her best to appear composed.

"You'll be glad to know," she said, "that your sneaky little plan has borne fruit. We've decided—" she smiled up at Dad – "to give it another go."

"Hooray!" Daisy clapped her hands and spun round in a circle.

"I thought you'd be pleased," said Mum. "They've been such miseries, I can't tell you! Talk about making a person feel guilty."

"Would you like us to go away again?" said Rose. "So that you can have a sort of second honeymoon?"

"Heaven forbid!" cried Mum. "The first one was bad enough!"

The four of them took up the story. It was one they had heard many times before.

"You didn't have any money—"

"So you decided to go camping."

"And Dad borrowed a tent—"

"Only it turned out to be an army bivouac."

"It was only meant for one person!"

"And it poured with rain the entire week."

"And every time one of you breathed, you touched the sides—"

"And all the rain came in!"

"And when you woke up, you were *soaking*."

"And guess who got the blame?" said Dad.

"*You did!*"

"Well, start as you mean to go on," said Mum. "Jazz, go and get some glasses. It's time for a toast! Your dad's brought a bottle of champagne."

"Can we all have some?" said Daisy.

"Yes! All of you!"

"Even me?" said Laurel.

"Well, if you can manage not to get roaring drunk," said Mum. She turned to Dad. "Do you know what this daughter of yours did? I took her to Rufus's party and—"

Laurel fled to the kitchen. "She's telling on me!" she wailed.

"That's good," said Jazz. "That's a good sign!"

Mum wanted to know what they should drink to.

"Someone propose a toast!"

It was Daisy who came up with the suggestion of happy families. Solemnly, they raised their glasses.

"Happy families!"

And also, Jazz couldn't help silently adding, "To drama school!"

She didn't mean to be selfish, but now that Dad was on telly…

"Before we go any further," said Dad. He pulled out his wallet and took out a sheet of paper. "I have a check list. I made a note, back at Christmas… let's see! One kitten, one computer, one new wardrobe, and one drama course. I can't quite remember who wanted what… who's the

156

boldest? Daisy! You must have been the drama course."

"No!" squealed Daisy, taking him seriously. "I was the kitten!"

"Were you, now? So who's the budding actress? Rose, was it you? Laurel, was it you? It can't have been Jazz! She's far too shy and retiring."

"Just like her dad," muttered Mum.

"Just like her mum," retorted Dad.

Jazz looked at Laurel: they grinned. Back on line!

"Mum, you're not *shy*," said Daisy.

"Well—" Mum shot Dad a little glance. "Only sometimes!"

"Jazz isn't ever," said Daisy. "That's why she's going to be a *star*."

"I'll drink to that," said Dad. He raised his glass, smiling at Jazz over the top of it. "To stardom!"

"To stardom," echoed Mum.

Help, thought Jazz, feeling her cheeks fire up.

"Look, look, she's turned all red!" gloated Laurel.

Jazz went into a mock swoon.

"It must be the drink," Jazz said. "It's gone to my head. You ought to know about *that*," she added to Laurel getting her own back.

"Girls, girls," said Mum. She held up her glass. Here's to happy families!"

Pumpkin Pie

This is the story of a drop-dead gorgeous girl
called Pumpkin, who has long blonde hair
and a figure to die for.
I wish!

It's my sister Petal who has the figure to die for. I'm the one in
the middle... the plump one. The other's the boy genius, my
brainy little brother, Pip. Then there's Mum, who's a high flier
and hardly ever around; and Dad, who's a chef. Dad really
loves to see me eat! I used to love to eat, too. I never wanted
food to turn into my enemy, but when Dad started calling me
Plumpkin I didn't feel I had any choice...

0 00 714392 3

Passion Flower

Of course, Mum shouldn't have
thrown the frying pan at Dad.
The day after she threw it,
Dad left home...

Stand back! Family Disaster Area! After the Frying Pan
Incident, it looks like me and the Afterthought are going
to be part of a single-parent family. Personally, I'm on Mum's
side but the Afterthought is Dad's number one fan. Typical.
Still, Dad's got us for the whole summer and things are
looking promising: no rules, no hassle, no worries.
But things never turn out the way you think.

0 00 715619 7

www.harpercollinschildrensbooks.co.uk
Visit the booklover's website